Love on the Boil

Neil S. Plakcy

Samwise Books

This book was originally published by Loose Id.

Edited by Maryam Salim.

What reviewers are saying about the series

"Neil Plakcy's *Mahu* series is a favorite of mine. His command of the local cultures and colloquialisms combined with strong characters and love of the island history has made that such a stunning series. Those strengths are on display [in the Love on series]." (Scattered Thoughts and Rogue Words review).

Chapter 1

Screwed the Pooch

The last time I saw Darren Carter, we had just finished a marathon fuck session to celebrate our college graduation. We'd been boyfriends for most of senior year, after meeting at a GLBT dance party, but we had both been avoiding the conversation about what would happen after commencement. I had already accepted a job on Wall Street, but I hadn't told Darren I'd be moving to New York.

I knew that he'd been interviewing for jobs and internships in his field, East Asia Studies, but he hadn't shared any results with me.

"I'm leaving for Japan tomorrow," he said, as I pulled out of his ass.

"That's what you were thinking about while we were fucking?" I asked. I peeled the condom off my dick and tossed it toward the trash can beside the bed. I missed, but I was too irritated to care. "The whole time we're doing it you're thinking about leaving me?"

"I wanted to tell you," he protested, as I stood up. He looked so sexy there, his skinny, hairless body covered with a sheen of sweat, a flop of brown hair over his forehead. "I could never figure out the right time."

"And this is the right time? While I've got your jizz all over my chest?"

Darren had come on me while I was making my final thrusts up his ass, and I could already feel a cold, clammy mess congealing among my chest hairs.

"Don't be such a drama queen," Darren said.

"Me!" I heard myself screech and made a conscious effort to dial it back. I was the stud, after all. The butch one nobody suspected was gay. I worked out and tended bar in the evenings. Darren was the queen who made a big deal out of everything.

"You're moving to New York anyway," Darren said. "Did you think I wouldn't find out?"

"Have you been reading my e-mails?"

"When you accessed your mail on my laptop the other day, you never logged out of your Gmail account. It popped up without my doing anything."

I pulled on my shorts and T-shirt without bothering to clean myself up. "So this is it? Thanks for the fuck; see you around?"

"You're the one who's always saying you don't want to get wrapped up in some heteronormative relationship," Darren said, sitting up against the pillows. "That we're just having fun together. What, did you think I was going to come to New York with you? We'd get an apartment in Brooklyn together? That I'd be your little woman, make you dinner every night?"

His words stung because I had been thinking that. Yeah, I didn't want to get wrapped up in anything too serious with Darren, wanted a chance to sow some wild oats and all that crap. God knew I'd fucked a lot of guys before him and figured there would be a lot more after him. But I always thought I'd be the one to end things, not Darren.

I stuck my feet into my deck shoes. "Have a good life," I said and I walked out the door.

I admit, I'd stalked him once or twice on social media over the last five years. Saw that he'd loved his postgrad year in Japan, how he'd moved to Portland for a job at a museum of Asian history. I'd gotten busy with my start-up and had no time for anything that wasn't work related or didn't lead to a quick fuck.

So I was stunned to see him in the reception area of Phil Sweet's office. Sweet was a venture capitalist I'd been courting for months, trying to get him to invest in my business. He'd asked me here for a face-to-face that I was sure was going to lead to a much-needed cash infusion.

A year before, I'd cashed out all my retirement savings and moved to Miami to start Cockteals, a business selling tea-based cocktail mixers to bars and restaurants. I wanted to start selling to the public too, but for that I needed cash to ramp up production and make distribution and advertising deals. I'd met Sweet at a venture hive event and intrigued him enough that we'd come this far together.

Seeing Darren in Sweet's lobby threw me for a loop. "Darren. What are you doing here?"

"I could ask you the same question."

He looked good. In the five years since graduation, he'd filled out a bit. His normally pale skin was tan, and I liked the way he'd cut his hair—very short on the sides, high and puffy on the top.

I noticed a tattoo on his right wrist—a tea cup. And then it clicked. "You have a tea business too?" I asked.

"What do you mean, too?"

Sweet's secretary opened the door behind the receptionist. "Mr. Sweet will see you both now."

Darren stood, and we followed the secretary to a conference room overlooking Lincoln Road, the pedestrian thoroughfare in the heart of Miami Beach. I'd spent a lot of time on that street over the past six months, talking to every restaurant and bar manager who'd meet with me. I was proud of the connections I'd made. I hoped Sweet was too.

Phil Sweet had been born under a lucky star. He'd majored in physics in college, and moved to Silicon Valley as the tech boom was beginning. He'd founded an Internet startup, which had eventually been acquired by one of the big players in online marketing. At that point, he'd cashed out and become a venture capitalist.

He was a tall, rangy guy with a perpetual tan that came from spending a lot of time on his hundred-foot yacht. He'd invested in a Miami company that taught coding to inner-city kids, and fallen in love with the weather and a gorgeous Cuban woman, so he'd relocated his business to Lincoln Road a year before.

He shook my hand and Darren's. "Darren Carter, meet Eddie Gonzalez," Sweet said.

"We've met," Darren said. "We went to college together."

"Oh yeah," Sweet said. "I knew that. But yours was a big class, wasn't it?"

"Two thousand. But Darren and I had some interests in common." I was feeling generous, so I added, "Darren's the one who introduced me to tea in the first place."

"Great. So you know about each other's businesses?"

"Nothing at all. We haven't been in touch since graduation," I said.

"Let's get reacquainted. Darren, you want to give your elevator pitch?"

I saw Darren gulp. He was an effusive guy, or at least he had been when I'd known him, but he was never comfortable giving presentations.

"Tea is one of the oldest beverages known to man, and one of the most versatile," he said. "But Americans have been slow to realize that. My company, DiversiTea, provides custom blends for upscale restaurants that complement the entrées and the desserts, as well as training wait staff on what to recommend."

Interesting. Darren and I were in the same market, though coming at it from different angles.

"Eddie?" Sweet asked.

"Like Darren, my company, Cockteals, aims at the higher-end restaurant market with custom tea blends used as the basis for high-end cocktails. I want to take my product line and introduce it to the consumer market."

"I want to do that too," Darren added.

"And that's why you're both here," Sweet said. "I'll be honest with you. There isn't room in my portfolio for two companies based in the same product. I love both your ideas and your enthusiasm, but I can't invest in both of you. And honestly, on your own, neither of you is strong enough. But if you work together—"

"No," Darren said.

"Absolutely not," I said, before I had the chance to think it through. There was no way I was going to be able to work with Darren.

Sweet shrugged. "Then our time here is done. I wish you both good luck."

And that was it. All that time struggling to make a connection with him, and Darren Carter had screwed the pooch in less than a minute.

Chapter 2

Over My Head

Eddie Fucking Gonzalez. Who'd have thought that he'd show up in Miami? Why wasn't he still some up-and-coming shark on Wall Street? And what the fuck was he doing with a tea business?

"We should talk," he said, as we walked out of Phil Sweet's office.

"About what? About how you just destroyed the last five years of my life?"

"Hey, you're the one who said no first," Eddie said.

I swallowed hard. He was right. I'd had a knee-jerk reaction to seeing him again. To how hot he still looked, his biceps bulging out of his short-sleeved shirt, the silky coating of dark hair on his arms, the faint hint of a five-o'clock shadow that reminded me how much I loved it when he rubbed his chin against my dick.

"I'll buy you a drink," Eddie said. "The Holding Company is one of my clients and they use my mixers in their Tea-Tinis."

"Holy shit. That's your business?" I asked as we walked outside. It was January and the digital readout on the clock tower said the temperature was seventy-two degrees. That reminded me of one more reason why I'd left the cold and damp of Portland to move to

Florida. That, and following Phil Sweet like an eager puppy waiting for a handout.

Eddie nodded. "You've had one?"

"I love those," I admitted. "Have you eaten at the Holding Company?"

"Yeah, I had dinner there a week ago." It was like a light bulb went on over Eddie's head. "Holy shit. I had a green hibiscus tea with dessert that was awesome. Was that your mix?"

I nodded. "I guess we do have something to talk about."

I was supposed to meet my boyfriend for dinner, but I texted him that some complications had come up with the deal, and I had to meet with someone to work things out. I said I'd explain later, though I wasn't sure I'd cough up that Eddie and I had been lovers in college. Parker was a good guy, and he wouldn't care, but I wasn't ready to get into any drama until I knew what was going to happen with the business deal.

Eddie and I stepped out onto Lincoln Road, past a beauty store specializing in mascara, concealer, and beehive wigs for drag queens. Next door was a restaurant run by Argentine immigrants featuring kosher vegan cuisine for the Orthodox Jewish women pushing strollers and trailed by little boys with curls hanging in front of their ears.

"Tell me about your business," I said to Eddie as we walked to the Holding Company.

"It all comes back to you," Eddie said, surprising me. "You and the tea."

When I was in high school, I did a class project on the Japanese tea ceremony, and that spurred my interest in different kinds of tea. By the time I met Eddie senior year, I had a shelf full of varieties of tea, a couple of types of infusers, and a big glass teapot. I used to experiment, mixing green, white, or black tea with different herbs and spices, and I remembered how excited I was to share my latest creation with Eddie, usually after a round of hot sex.

"Yeah, blame it on me," I said lightly.

"I do. When I got to New York, I missed all the tea you used to make, so I went looking for it. One night I was fooling around, and I poured some bourbon into a cup of Earl Grey. It was like this door opened, you know?"

"I know," I said.

The restaurants along Lincoln Road had overtaken the center median, the only distinction between them the color of the big café umbrellas and the shape of the tables. Maroon umbrellas shaded square wooden tables; dark green protected round tables with white cloths, yellow over long communal wooden tables and hard chairs that kept patrons from lingering too long.

The traffic enforcement cops rode modified stand-up scooters. The cross streets were filled with lumbering tour buses and handicap-access vans, low-slung convertibles and tiny European imports.

"I got obsessed, figuring out how to mix different kinds of tea with rum or bourbon or vodka or tequila," Eddie said. "My fridge filled up with containers of simple syrup in all different tea flavors. When I went out drinking with guys from work, I'd carry a thermos with me with one of the syrups. I'd order a shot of something and make my own drink."

"This is while you were working on Wall Street?"

"Yeah, I was a financial analyst. Learned a shitload about what makes a company tick. Earned a lot of money, which I socked away."

We approached the restaurant, and both of us reached to hold the door open for the other. Oh yeah, I remembered. That had been our dynamic in college—both of us wrestling to be the alpha male in the relationship. Because I liked to bottom for Eddie, he thought that meant he was in charge of everything—which pissed me off royally.

Fortunately, there were two doors to the Holding Company, and we each went in one of them. The walls were decorated with business memorabilia from the past—stock certificates from companies that had crashed at the end of the Jazz Age, fedoras that might have been worn by characters on *Mad Men,* tickertape machines that had once spit out the fortunes of a country.

Eddie and I both knew the hostess, a voluptuous Latina named Veronica, and she hugged us both. Me first, which satisfied me in a perverse way.

She led us to a table, and we settled down. I decided to be the bigger man and ask Eddie which of his cocktails he'd recommend.

"You still like salty things?" Eddie asked. "I remember for a while you were living on those soft pretzels from the vendor on Walnut Street."

I was surprised that Eddie remembered. Sometimes on his way over to my apartment from class he'd stop and buy me a pretzel with mustard, and I devoured that salty goodness and let him have his way with me.

"Sure," I said, swallowing hard.

"Try the chamomile tequila sour." I recognized that devilish grin. "I want to see you lick the salt off the rim of the glass."

My dick began to stiffen at the innuendo, but I tried to ignore it. "And what are you going to have?"

"I prefer my drinks and my men sweet," he said, and that grin reached up to his eyes. "I'll have a bourbon half and half."

We ordered our drinks. "So," I said. "You were working on Wall Street, mixing up your own tea cocktails."

He nodded. "One day a bartender buddy of mine asked me what the hell I was doing, and I showed him. He loved the drink I made, told his boss, and that started my business. My buddy didn't want to mess with brewing the tea and making the syrup himself, so every week I'd make up a half-dozen different batches, bottle them up, and drop them off."

"You did all that yourself?"

Eddie nodded. "For the first few months. I bought cartons of bottles online, had a gal I worked with design a logo for me and print me labels. It was a shitload of work."

"I know exactly what you're talking about."

The server delivered our cocktails, and I lifted mine to my lips. I smelled the distinctive aroma of chamomile, and loved the way the herb interacted with the tequila. "This is awesome," I said. Then, because I couldn't help myself, I licked some of the salt off the rim and was rewarded by seeing a flash of hunger in Eddie's eyes.

He put down his drink and cleared his throat. "Eventually I found this company in Brooklyn that would do the brewing and bottling for me. My buddy moved to a different bar, a chain, and he introduced me there. Pretty soon I had to hire a guy to pick up the bottles of syrup and deliver them to the bars. And thus was born a business."

He sat back in his chair, and I knew from long experience that he was using that opportunity to adjust himself in his pants. So Eddie still had a thing for me. Hmm.

"What's your story?" he asked.

"Spent the year after college in Japan. Interned for a while with a tea company that specialized in growing green tea and grinding it for *matcha* the way they've been doing for centuries. Came back to the States and got a low-level job at a museum in Portland. Hated it, and when the matcha company decided to expand to the States, I jumped on as a sales rep for the northwest region. I hit the ground as people started discovering how cool matcha is, all the health benefits, the way you can use it in recipes."

The server returned, and we ordered another round of drinks and the antipasto plate to nibble on while we talked and drank.

"I'd travel around selling tea to specialty stores, and I'd eat in these great restaurants, and after the meal I'd ask about tea and they'd often bring out one of those wooden boxes, like it was a special thing, but inside would be the same old bags of Earl Grey, Orange Pekoe. And nobody knew which tea to recommend to go with whatever you were having for dessert, or to follow up on your meal."

Eddie nodded. "I've seen the same thing."

The platter arrived laden with roasted tomatoes, tiny bites of salami, and wedges of focaccia. As I expected, Eddie jumped on the marinated artichoke hearts. I was happy to let him have them as long as I could eat the prosciutto and melon. "Like old times," I said, remembering the platters we'd shared at an Italian place a couple of blocks off campus.

"With higher-end ingredients."

"And higher prices."

"So you decided to do something about the lack of tea knowledge in restaurants," Eddie said.

"I did. At first I was trying to sell Mizumi's tea to some of these places, teaching how to brew it, what to recommend it with. I remembered there was a whole world of tea flavor out there, and I started coming up with custom mixes of tea leaves and herbs and spices. Like you, I began by doing the packaging myself but very quickly I got in over my head."

Eddie looked at me and that old familiar gleam was in his eyes, the one that in the past had always led us into bed. Was I getting in over my head once again?

Chapter 3

Smell

Hanging out with Darren was so awesome that it washed away any bad feelings I'd harbored about our breakup. We talked for hours that evening, through cocktails, the antipasto platter, entrées and dessert, accompanied by Darren's custom-mixed tea. I was impressed at how well the server was able to explain the differences to us. Darren had trained him and his colleagues well.

The alarm on my watch beeped, and I remembered I'd made a plan to hook up with a guy I'd met online.

Fortunately, we'd arranged to meet at a gay bar on Lincoln Road, a few blocks from Sweet's office. I figured we'd share a drink, swap some spit, and head to my apartment for a fuck session. But first I had to say good-bye to Darren.

I motioned to the server for the check, and we each handed him a credit card with instructions to split the bill.

"This has been great, catching up on old times," I said. "But we should plan a regular business meeting soon, see if there is synergy between our two operations and if we can work together the way Phil Sweet wants."

"You think we can? Work together, I mean?"

"Why not? Our products are complementary. I'm before dinner, you're after dinner. We obviously cater to the same kind of restaurant clients, and if I get the cash from Sweet to expand to the consumer market, I can pull you along with me."

"I've already got plans for that," Darren said.

"All the more reason why we should work together."

He frowned.

"What?" I asked. "What's the problem? You think we'll end up in the sack together again? Tell me you don't want that anyway."

"Fuck you and your ego, Eddie," Darren said. "I have a boyfriend. I want to focus on my business. No distractions. And how do I know I can trust you?"

"Jesus. You trusted me to bareback with you a couple of times, didn't you? You can't get more trust than that."

The server chose that moment to return with our cards and receipts, and I felt my face redden. When he was gone, Darren said, "That attitude is exactly why I can't work with you. You want to do everything your way. This is my business, Eddie. Mine. You're not going to take it away from me."

He scrawled a signature on the receipt, then pushed his chair back with a loud scrape and stood up. "This is clearly not going to work. Good luck with your business."

He stalked out of the restaurant, and even though I was boiling mad at him I couldn't help noticing the way his black slacks hugged his bubble butt—the butt I'd enjoyed plowing so much, back in the day.

I was still pissed off as I strode toward Splash. Backpack-laden tourists trudging along Lincoln Road determined to have fun even if their legs ached and sweat dripped down their foreheads. A teen girl was so entranced with her smartphones that she bumped into a pair of Latin men in sleek black suits and thousand-dollar loafers and didn't even excuse herself.

The night had cooled down, and I wished I'd brought a jacket with me. But what the hell, I'd be warming up fast with my hookup.

I walked in the door to the bar and looked around. The place was packed with men with shaved heads, with artfully messy bed-head, with backward ball caps, with extravagant dreadlocks. Guys in skinny jeans, in fishing shirts and denim shorts, in oversize Dolphins T-shirts and bathing trunks. Older men in plain white T-shirts and knee-length camouflage shorts. Crew-cut college jocks in muscle shirts, black guys with arms covered in tattoos.

I finally spotted my guy. He'd said his name was Luis, that he was thirty-two, Colombian, and into oral and bottoming. Right up my alley. Unfortunately, it was clear that his picture had been Photoshopped, wiping out the acne scars on his chin, filling in some of his hair, and reducing the size of his belly. But what the hell—I wasn't planning to marry him, just fuck him into a stupor.

He seemed to get off on the anger at Darren that was still radiating from me. We had one round of beer, and then he pulled me over to the wall and started to kiss me, openmouthed like he wanted to swallow me up. Yeah, he was oral all right.

For a moment I wished he was someone different, someone like Darren, maybe one of those cute guys with neatly trimmed beards, flannel shirts, and jeans, who worked at one of the Internet startups and lived on expensive sushi and Starbucks lattes.

But Luis was there and clearly into me, and I wasn't going to walk away. I ground my pelvis into him as we sucked face, and I swear I might have come right there if he hadn't pulled back and said, "I want you to fuck me. You said you live around here?"

"I do." I grabbed his hand, and we hurried out of the bar past an elderly woman with a gold lamé handbag, matching pumps, and sunglasses big enough to cover her entire face.

It was bad luck, I guess, that we ran right into Darren Carter, holding hands with a stocky dude with a blond crew cut. "Motherfucker," I grumbled. I totally ignored Darren, tugging Luis along.

It wasn't far to my apartment, in a high-rise on Purdy Avenue overlooking Biscayne Bay, but by the time we got there my hard-on had deflated, and I wondered what the fuck I was doing with this anonymous trick. Luis hadn't lost the urge, though, and as soon as we got into my apartment, he was pulling his clothes off like a man possessed.

I was subletting a small studio from the cousin of a guy I knew in New York, and so my bed wasn't far. Luis scrambled over there and climbed onto all fours, his hairy butt facing me. "Come on, *mi amor*, what are you waiting for?" he asked.

"Nothing at all," I said, feeling my anger at Darren return. I stripped down while Luis fingered his hole with lube, and then I rolled on a condom and lined myself up behind him.

Darren Carter, I thought, Darren Carter, making a rhythm out of the syllables. Push in on the Dar, back out on ren. In on Car, back on ter. Who did he think he was, anyway, ruining my chance to get venture capital funding? He couldn't trust me? Ha! How could I trust him, when he'd never bothered to mention he was leaving me for Japan?

Luis got into my rhythm, pushing back against me as I went deeper and deeper into him, so that my balls were slapping against his ass and my dickhead pushed against his prostate again and again. He moaned in pleasure, but I wasn't feeling it. His ass was as wide as the Holland Tunnel, and he smelled funky—a mix of cologne, sweat, and shit. I wanted to get off and get rid of him, but my dick wasn't cooperating.

"Oh, yeah, fuck my ass," he panted. "You're so good."

I could do without the cheesy porn-film dialogue. I squeezed my eyes shut and focused on Darren Carter. We were back at the Holding Company, and I'd pushed him facedown on the table, dragging his pants down and exposing his sweet, sexy ass. He'd gone commando to dinner, knowing what I wanted to do, and I got down on my knees and began to lick his ass. It tasted like chamomile tea, sweet with a sharp kick, and he moaned with pleasure as I tongue fucked him.

All the time I was fantasizing, I kept plowing Luis's ass, but my heart wasn't in it, though he was clearly getting off on me. I reached around and started to jerk him as I finally felt my orgasm rising, and he came a moment before I did, babbling in high-pitched Spanish.

I pulled out of him and collapsed on the carpet. I didn't even want to climb up onto the bed and lie there next to him—I was already plotting how quickly I could get rid of him.

"You are some fuck, Señor Gonzales," he said, giving my name the Spanish pronunciation, softening the z the way my Cuban-born *abuelo* had.

Great. Now I was feeling like I'd just fucked my grandfather. Big ick.

I forced myself to my feet. I pulled the slimy condom off and tossed it into the trash. My comforter smelled like cum and sweat. At least there was a washer-dryer down the hall. "Sorry, gotta say good-bye," I said to Luis as he lay there on my bed. "I've got a big day tomorrow at work, and I need some rest."

It took a few more minutes of manipulating and cajoling before he dressed and left, extracting a promise to do this again soon. A promise I had no intention of keeping. I bundled up the comforter and tossed it in the laundry basket, then went into the shower, where I scrubbed myself clean.

No matter how hard I tried, though, I couldn't get the scent out of my nostrils. Not of Luis or his stinky butt—but of Darren Carter.

Fuck me.

Chapter 4

Choice

"Do you know that guy?" Parker asked me, as Eddie and his trick of the moment swept past us. "Because he looked at you like he wanted to kill you."

"It's a long story," I said.

"I'm a good listener."

He was. Parker was a social worker who counseled at-risk teenagers about HIV. A good guy, who'd had a rough time coming out in a family of evangelical Christians in Massachusetts. He had found salvation in a youth group, and been so impressed with what the counselors did that he majored in social work and wanted to devote his life to making other people happy.

Weirdly, that was one of the things about him that bothered me the most. He was so selfless, so saintly, that I could never get a rise out of him. He acceded to anything I wanted to do, and that evening, he'd willingly come to meet me on Lincoln Road when he sensed my agitation after my dinner with Eddie.

We moved slowly down Lincoln Road, past hunky guys on roller skates zigzagging around older gay couples with tiny dogs on bright red leashes that flashed in the evening darkness, sweating tourists talking animatedly in Russian peppered with occasional mentions of Miami Bitch and Sawgrass Mills, and a man in Speedos, his whole body painted silver, who performed robotic dances to the songs of one-hit wonders from the 1980s.

"He's the guy I had dinner with," I said. "My ex-boyfriend from college."

"The one who ditched you when you went to Japan?"

"We ditched each other." I still felt prickly about the way things had ended between us. I should have told him about the study-abroad scholarships I was applying for, and he should have told me about the jobs he interviewed for in New York. We both should have been a lot more honest with each other.

That was a pattern I wasn't going to repeat with Parker. As we walked, I told him everything.

Well, not exactly everything. Not how good the sex was with Eddie, or how complete I felt when I was with him. I stuck to the basics—dated, broke up, both started businesses, brought together by Phil Sweet.

"What a small world it is," Parker said.

"I guess. I mean, I'm the one who got him into tea in the first place. But it is weird that both of us would turn to entrepreneurship, and in the tea world."

"You must have had a great effect on him," Parker said. "I can see that. You're a very persuasive, powerful individual."

Sometimes I wanted to shake him. I'd confessed to having dinner with my ex-boyfriend, and Parker didn't seem to have an iota of jealousy.

Was that a good thing, or a bad one? Maybe he was such a good person that he assumed the best of everyone. Or maybe he didn't care enough for me to be jealous.

His hand began to feel clammy, and I pulled mine free, pretending I needed to adjust my hair. Parker didn't seem to mind. Nor was he upset when I told him that I was tired after the long day.

"Can we skip you coming back to my place? I need to chill and think through these business problems."

"Whatever you need. Sometimes the most important thing we can do for ourselves is spend time on our own."

Yeah, thanks for the social-worker insight into my behavior. I kissed him good-bye and turned back toward the garage where I'd parked before the meeting with Phil Sweet. Darkness had fallen and the street was lit by neon chopsticks from the Brazilian-Japanese sushi bar, the overly bright window displays at the store catering to tourists who'd forgotten to bring sunglasses for the tropical sun, the spangled snowflakes hanging from light poles as a way to bring winter to the land of endless sunshine.

I realized with a pang that I missed my home town in Ohio. The nip in the air in late October as we decorated our house with skeletons and pumpkins and sheaves of parti-colored Indian corn. The first dusting of white that made our ordinary backyard look like Narnia after the kids went through the wardrobe, as if there might be a faun in a knitted scarf hiding behind a tree. Lying on my back in a drift of fresh snow, waving my arms to make a snow angel.

In college, the change of the seasons meant adding and removing layers, pairing a jewel-toned polo shirt with a pale blue oxford-cloth button-down and a nubby crew-necked wool sweater. I had a collection of scarves in colors and patterns—ghosts and goblins for Halloween, buckle-hatted pilgrims and plump turkeys for Thanksgiving, Santa's sleigh filled with presents, Valentine hearts and cupids.

I missed wearing those scarves. The closest I got to winter in South Florida was entering an overly air-conditioned movie theater or restaurant. Most of the time, like that evening as I reached the bus stop, I was sweating even in the lightest-weight shirt.

At least the bus was air-conditioned, and I rode up Collins Avenue to the apartment I was renting mid-Beach, in a working-class neighborhood of Hispanic families. My neighbors were surprised that I lived by myself—didn't I have family to take care of? All of them seemed to be sharing with grandparents and cousins and in-laws along with lots of little kids.

I walked to my building, a three-story low-rise built in the 1950s, with no architectural distinction whatsoever. As I approached I heard, as usual, Latin music playing somewhere, which reminded me of what Eddie had introduced me to in college. The five-stroke pattern of the rhumba and the conga, the fast-paced habanera, the percussive beat of Afro-Cuban jazz. I remembered Eddie dancing the mambo in my apartment one night during senior year, the way his hips moved as if his body was made of liquid, not bone. He'd tried to teach me those dances, but I was an Ohio boy without the rhythm that had been born into him.

When I got into my apartment, the music still reverberated through the paper-thin walls of my apartment, and I'd grown accustomed to working with headphones on. I plugged in and turned to a collection of Jake Shimabukuro's ukulele recordings whose melodies, seemingly simple but ultimately quite complex, reminded me of the koto music I'd come to love in Japan.

With the ukulele soaring and falling in my ears, I looked at my latest spreadsheet. I was making money, barely, because I hadn't reached a sales volume yet that would let me take advantage of economies of scale. I'd hoped the influx of capital from Phil Sweet would help with that, as well as funding my living expenses while I devoted myself completely to the business.

What was I going to do without that money? I'd solicited a dozen venture capitalists from Silicon Valley to Wall Street, and Sweet was the only one who'd expressed any interest at all. I'd met him at an incubator event in Portland, and we'd clicked. He loved to drink tea and recognized that my products reached a niche that hadn't been served yet.

We had corresponded for several months, and at one point he'd mentioned that it was a shame I was on the other side of the country. If I was closer to him, we might be able to meet occasionally.

By that time I'd broken up with a Japanese-American guy I was dating in Portland, my lease was coming up, and I realized I had no ties keeping me from moving to Florida.

So I did.

Sweet had been as good as his word. Once a month I'd met with him, and he'd helped me develop the spreadsheets I was staring at. To understand investment terms, to translate my passion for tea into something that could be a real business. And in one rash moment, I'd wiped out a year of work.

There was no way my business was sustainable at this level. I'd already used up most of the cash I'd put aside from my jobs. I had some small income from a regular column I wrote for my old employer's newsletter, but that barely covered my rent. The problem with my business model, Sweet had pointed out, was that I introduced restaurant to tea pairings and taught their staff for free, depending on revenue from selling them my custom blends to make a profit. There wasn't enough volume coming from my existing clients, so I was constantly on the prowl for new business.

Most of my time was spent on non-revenue-generating activities, like researching and pitching restaurants. I needed to break into the consumer market to develop a steadier stream of income. But I couldn't do that without an infusion of capital.

I kept coming back to my meeting that afternoon with Phil and Eddie. If I hadn't been blindsided, I might have been more thoughtful in considering the deal. Could I work with Eddie? Could we both overcome the sexual tension between us to focus on making money together?

Did I have any other choice?

I remembered that Eddie's business was called Cockteals, and I looked up his website. It was pretty professional looking—better than mine, which I'd had a teenaged coder in Portland build for me on the cheap. I clicked on the *contact us* link and took a deep breath.

We should talk, I typed. I added my cell number, my e-mail and my website address. Before I could second-guess myself, I clicked Send.

Chapter 5

Taste

I wasn't surprised to get the e-mail from Darren. I had the sense that he needed me more than I needed him. He'd revealed the problems with his current business model, the way he gave away so much for free in order to establish customer accounts, and I knew that he couldn't sustain that forever.

We met at a Starbucks on Lincoln Road. I ordered us both the green tea and doctored it up with a dose of hibiscus and rose petal simple syrup from a hip flask. We sat beside each other at a big table, our laptops in front of us, but before we could start crunching numbers, we had to talk big picture.

"I'm thinking a joint venture to approach the consumer market," I said. "You retain your existing restaurant business and so do I, but we each contribute our intellectual property to the new venture. We can monetize those assets through production and mass-market distribution."

"I love it when you talk Wall Street," Darren said drily. "I'm not sure that's going to work, though." He picked up the green tea I'd doctored for him and sipped it. "This is good."

"I know. Why won't my plan work?"

"Because there's a big difference between what we do now and what we want to do. When you sell your Tea-Tini mixes, you go to the bartenders and explain how to make the drinks. I do the same thing with my custom tea blends. I have twenty-four blends right now —way too many to start a consumer brand with. I'll bet you have a lot of mixers too."

"You're right. We're going to have to cherry-pick the product line."

"And we have to consider shelf life and storage considerations."

I groaned. I'd been so caught up in thinking about the economic angles I'd forgotten about the products.

We spent the next two hours getting technical. Which mixes had the broadest appeal? Which had the greatest shelf life and least chance of spoiling? "You know people aren't going to follow the directions," Darren said. "They'll open a box of tea and let moisture get in. Then they'll try it a year later and complain that the flavor is gone."

"Or they'll use cheap booze with my mixers and wonder why the drink doesn't taste the way it did in the restaurant."

We decided the most efficient way to choose products would be to set up a tasting, invite all our friends, and see what response we got. But before that, we'd need to taste-test everything ourselves.

"Come over to my apartment tomorrow," Darren said. "We'll brew up a bunch of teas and test them."

"I'll bring my mixers and booze," I said. I was glad that we were going to Darren's place—my studio would be uncomfortably small for the two of us. Then again, I had no idea what kind of apartment Darren had.

"You drive back and forth to get here?" I asked, when he gave me his address.

He shook his head. "Can't afford the parking. I take the bus. Runs right up Collins."

I wasn't about to take the bus myself, especially not if I had to carry a lot of material up to Darren's apartment, so the next afternoon I drove up there. It was only a couple of miles from South Beach, but a world away. Though the art deco architecture was similar, lots of low-rise buildings with those eyebrow windows, there were no high-rises, and the restaurants along Collins Avenue were small and ethnic —Brazilian, Colombian, takeout pizza, and bars with old-fashioned neon beer signs in the windows. Not a market for tea-tinis or custom tea blends.

When I got close to his place, I realized there was no way I was finding a convenient parking spot, so I called and asked him to come down and carry up some of my stuff. "There's an alley behind my building where you can park," he said. "Turn left on Seventy-Eighth and right on Byron and I'll meet you back there."

He was standing along the building as I crept along the alley, avoiding trash bins and parked cars. "Pull right in here," he said, pointing to a narrow spot parallel to the building. "It's the super's space, and he's out of town for the week."

I pulled in and got the plastic bin where I kept my demo bottles of liquor and simple syrup out of the trunk. I often took it around to restaurants to show what the bartenders could do with my mixes, and I reminded myself this was just another demonstration. Even though Darren looked damn sexy in a pair of tight shorts and a tank top emblazoned with a picture of a beach and the logo, *Right here is good.*

All he needed was to flip the shirt around and draw an arrow pointing to his ass, and I'd be happy to oblige.

I shook that thought off, though. Darren and I were going to be business partners, not fuck buddies. I had apps for that.

I followed Darren up a set of stairs, trying to avoid noting the way his ass moved as he climbed. His apartment was a small one-bedroom with a window out onto the back alley, but at least we didn't have a bed right in front of us as we got set up, as we would have had if he'd come to my place.

He had the same fussy routine for brewing tea that I remembered from college. Start with cold spring or purified water. Bring to a gentle boil and test the temperature with a thermometer. Each variety of tea, from green to black, needed to be prepared at a particular temperature.

"There is no way you're getting ordinary customers to test the temperature of their water," I said, as I watched Darren work. "You're going to have to get around that."

"I include instructions in the packages I sell to restaurants," he said. "There's nothing wrong with giving those to consumers too."

Yeah, right, I thought, as he set a small timer beside a glass pot of green tea. Each variety needed a different amount of time to steep as well. There was no way we were going to be able to convince people to follow these intricate directions.

"The tea will be fine if you break the rules," Darren said, as if he was reading my mind. "We're talking about optimum conditions now."

The more I thought about it, the more his business seemed to suit Darren. He was fussy that way, an elderly man in a young guy's body. Everything had to be just so. As I looked around his apartment I saw his Japanese fixation clearly. A single futon in the living room, with a Hokusai reproduction positioned exactly above it. His glass-fronted kitchen cabinets were neatly organized, and everything was sparkling clean.

Not the way I lived at all. My studio was jammed with souvenirs, and the posters on my walls hung haphazardly. My kitchen was clean, sure, but not immaculate like Darren's. And while I did have a couple of different teapots and infusers, they were all jumbled together in one cabinet.

When Darren leaned over to serve me my first cup of green tea, his tank top ballooned out, and I got a glimpse of his dark nipples, each surmounting a caramel-colored areola. My mouth watered as I imagined taking them in, licking and sucking and nibbling until Darren squirmed in pleasure beneath me.

I blew out a long breath and focused on the tea. We tasted a dozen different blends, nibbling on bland crackers and swigging cold water between each to clear our palates. Even with the old-fashioned window air conditioner working nonstop, we both got hot and sweaty, and as Darren stood at the stove brewing what had to be our ninth or tenth tasting, I couldn't help noticing the way his nylon shorts puckered in at his ass, and see the sweat dripping from his back to his crack.

The heat was a stimulus to my libido and I kept having to adjust my dick in my shorts as it hardened and pressed painfully against the fabric. Darren didn't say anything, but I knew he had to be feeling it too. "You mind if I take my shirt off?" I asked as I began to unbutton it.

"I do mind, actually," Darren said.

"Why? My sexy chest going to make you do something crazy?"

"I have a boyfriend, remember? And don't you?"

"Me? No."

"Who was that guy I saw you with coming out of Splash yesterday?"

"A trick, Darren. A guy I met online, had a drink with, fucked, then said good-bye to. It's called dating."

"No, it's called being a slut. And even if I didn't have Parker, I wouldn't want any part of that."

"Parker? As in Parker House Rolls?"

"No, as in Parker, a sweet guy who treats me like a king."

He plopped the next cup of tea down in front of me so that a bit of tea slopped over the rim of the cup. That had to make him crazy.

"This is white tea flavored with orange peel and a smidgen of dried coconut."

I picked up the glass and took a sip. "Tastes like my coconut orange daiquiri blend," I said, after letting the tea sit in my mouth for a moment, savoring the different flavors.

"I didn't copy from you. Hell, I didn't even know you were doing tea until yesterday."

"Calm down. I wasn't saying you were copying from me. Just that great minds think alike. I think this could be a keeper."

"They're all keepers," he grumbled, but he sat down across from me and sipped the tea. "It is pretty good."

"The tang of the orange and the sweetness of the coconut balance each other, and they're flavors most people are familiar with and like. My daiquiri mix is one of the most popular across the board."

We went back to polite tasting, but the tension between us hung in the hot, humid air. Was it sexual tension or conflict that arose from trying to blend two different business ideas together?

By the time we were done, we had narrowed the range down to three that had the greatest difference in flavor profile—a green mixed with hibiscus and ginger, the coconut-orange white, and a black that was sweet and rich, with a hint of raspberry. I was impressed by the way the elements worked together, attacking the taste buds so that the final experience was all-encompassing.

Then it was my turn. While Darren stood at the sink washing teapots and cups, I laid out bottles of rum, vodka, tequila, and bourbon. I started with the coconut orange daiquiri I'd mentioned before, and Darren agreed with me that the flavors in his tea were very similar. "I could drink a couple of these and not even notice," he said.

That was high praise. I used a rasp to shave ice cubes for a vodka, strawberry, and white tea snow cone. I added fresh sprigs of mint from my kitchen garden to a mint julep infused with Kentucky bourbon and mint tea. Darren laughed. "You complain about my products needing specific instructions, and you expect some customer to shave ice with a—what is that, some industrial tool?"

"It's a rasp," I said. "A lot of guys will already have them, if they do any woodworking."

He snorted. "Yeah, there's probably a huge intersection between guys who do woodworking and those who drink Japanese tea. Like, maybe you, and a bear in Seattle."

"Ha-ha. Taste the damn drink."

He sipped it. "Wow. It feels like being a kid with an adult beverage."

"And there's sure as hell a market for that," I said. I had brought a range of different glasses, and as the afternoon wore on, they lined up on Darren's kitchen counter like fallen soldiers.

By the time we had run through my whole product line, we were both tipsy, even though I'd tried to keep our intake to tastes. That earlier tension had worn off, and we were laughing a lot and touching each other casually. I was getting hella horny and calculating how quickly I could find a hookup to relieve myself when Darren said, "I'm starving. Want to order a pizza?"

That sounded like a better idea than driving in my current state, so we did. He remembered my preference for sausage, and he kept the green peppers he liked to one half of the pizza. No vegetation for me—I was strictly carnivorous when it came to pizza. He put some cool instrumental music on the stereo, and we laughed and talked about old friends and old times. We sat across from each other at the kitchen table to eat, and my foot rubbed against his in the way it had in the past.

We both kept drinking the cocktails too, and even with the pizza to absorb some of the alcohol, we were giddy. "There's no way you can drive home," Darren said eventually. "You'll have to stay here."

I was ready to agree eagerly until he added, "The futon folds out into a bed."

"What would Parker House Rolls say about that?"

"He trusts me," Darren said defensively.

"And you trust me?"

"You know, you're right. I'll call you an Uber. You can pick up your car tomorrow."

I blew out a long breath. "I'm being an asshole. You're very gracious to offer me your futon and if I haven't completely pissed you off, I'll accept."

Darren looked at me, and I held my breath until he said yes.

Chapter 6

Sweat

Inviting Eddie to stay at my apartment was a colossal mistake. As I lay in bed in my boxers, I kept expecting him to barge into my bedroom naked, wagging that big dick I remembered so well. The worst part was that somewhere in the darkest recesses of my libido I wanted him to.

The air conditioner in my bedroom window wheezed and hummed so I couldn't hear anything from the living room. Was Eddie already asleep? Was he lying there like I was?

I wanted to taste him again, smell him, feel him inside me. But I couldn't do that to Parker, who was a sweet guy who cared for me. He'd dated a couple of cheaters in the past, and I knew he was hypersensitive on that issue. It would destroy him if I gave in to my carnal impulses with Eddie Gonzalez.

I turned onto my side, then turned again. My dick was hard, and eventually I gave in, threw off the sheets, and pulled down my boxers. I ran my thumb over the head of my stiff dick, spreading the precum around, rubbing that sensitive spot below the slit.

I closed my eyes and imagined that was Eddie's hand on my dick instead of my own. With my other hand I rubbed my left tit until it was hard and swollen. I began to stroke my dick up and down, using my thumb. I wasn't one of those guys who could fist his dick fast—I had to go slow, letting those blood vessels swell, feeling the pressure start to churn in my gut, the endorphins rise through my system.

Eddie knew that. He was a master of the slow boil, bringing me up, keeping me poised at the edge of that cliff, longing for sweet release but knowing that it would be over all too soon so I needed to savor the moment.

At least, he'd known that, back in college. Who knew how he fucked now, five years later, after untold lips had caressed his dick, untold dicks gone down his throat or up his ass? I pictured Eddie in those glorious moments after sex, his cheeks reddened, a drop of sweat on his forehead, a satisfied smirk on his lips. Quickly I was flying on the wings of an orgasm so strong that it shook my entire body. I hadn't come like that in years. Since the last time I'd had sex with Eddie?

For a couple of minutes, I lay there, catching my breath and letting the endorphins rage through my body like warriors returning from battle. Then I slept.

I woke as the first fingers of dawn crept through my window, a clear white light that made me embarrassed about what I'd done the night before. I lay there in bed for a while, repeating all the reasons why it was a bad idea to get sexy with Eddie Gonzalez. I finally gave up, motivated myself to get up, clean up, and put on running shorts and a clean tank top.

Eddie was sitting up on the futon, the covers down low enough to show the wild thatch of dark curls below his belly button. I realized that he'd slept in the nude, the way he had back in college, and my dick stiffened at the memory.

I turned toward the door so Eddie wouldn't see my hard-on. "I'm going for a run along the beach," I said. "You can shower if you want. I have a key—just pull the door closed after you and it'll lock."

"I could come with you," Eddie said. "You have some gear I could borrow?"

My first thought was that if we ran together and he left, I'd have his sweaty clothes to jerk off against later. I swallowed hard. "I'll get you something." I turned back, and I was sure in that moment that he saw my stiff dick tenting my shorts, and I pictured the straight porn I occasionally stumbled past on the Internet, the big-boobed women with their hands in their snatch, and my dick wilted.

Eddie was stockier than I was, but I had an oversize T-shirt he could wear and a pair of shorts that were too big on me. I even had a jockstrap he could wear.

"This was my jock," he said, holding it up. "Did you keep it all these years?"

"That's not yours," I protested.

"It's exactly the brand I wore in college."

He pushed aside the rest of the covers and stood up. My mouth went dry as he stepped into the jock. His body was even lusher than I remembered, a broad chest that tapered to a narrow waist, his beefy dick half-hard as it nestled in a forest of pubic hair.

"Maybe it wasn't mine after all," he said, as he stuffed his junk into the pouch, and the strap rested low on his abdomen. "Either that or I've put on weight since college."

"It looks good on you," I said. I realized I was staring, and I tossed him the shirt and shorts. "Get dressed and let's get moving."

We hurried down the stairs to the front door of my building and stepped out into a wave of heat and humidity. We started out at a slow lope east on Seventy-Eight Street to warm up, moving easily past a Latina pushing a double stroller, a boy and girl who looked like twins or were at least dressed that way. Men in bathing suits with towels draped over their shoulders on their way to the beach, and an old woman in a wheelchair being pushed by her aide.

We had to stop and wait for a break in traffic to cross Harding Street, then stop again at Collins Avenue. We passed maids coming home from night shifts in their faded blue and white uniforms, a couple of black teenagers with dreadlocks, an elderly woman pushing a three-wheeled cart loaded with groceries from Publix.

It felt like old times to be with Eddie—and though I knew that was dangerous, it was also incredibly seductive. Finally, we were at the entrance to the park, where white sugar sand stretched on either side of the narrow paved path that led toward the beach, crisscrossed by fat tire tracks of beach maintenance vehicles.

Dead sea grape leaves littered the pavement, along with empty Marlboro packs and crushed chip bags. We turned south onto the paved path and jogged in easy rhythm, past a series of multimillion-dollar properties, single-family homes that ranged from ultra-modern to Mediterranean revival with coral tile roofs and twisted white columns.

I'd jogged past there a dozen times but never stopped to consider living in one of those houses. That kind of money was beyond me, wasn't it?

Unless this new joint venture with Eddie took off. I'd read hundreds of articles of entrepreneurs who'd created businesses in their garages and sold them off for millions. Maybe one day I'd be able to buy a place like this, with lots of bedrooms for my adopted children, an infinity pool in the backyard.

High-rise condos rose ahead of us, beyond a line of tall palm trees. The sun glimmered in a lemon-yellow ball over sparkling blue-green water to our right, beyond the grassy dunes.

We sprinted for a while, Eddie keeping pace with me, and we ran the length of the park, about nine blocks, then turned around and ran back. By the time we got back to my apartment, we were both panting and drenched in sweat.

"You can go into the shower first," I said. "You've probably got work to do today."

"We could go in together. Save water and all that."

"Are you ever going to let up?" I asked. "Jesus, what made me think I could ever work with you? I can imagine we'd be in a meeting with Phil Sweet, and you'd be trying to feel me up under the table, follow me into the men's room."

"You'd like that, wouldn't you?"

It killed me that I would. What kind of a jerk was I, to be thinking of cheating on sweet Parker with the guy who'd already broken my heart once? I took a deep breath. "You should go, Eddie. And we should both consider whether we can work together."

"Your loss." He pulled my T-shirt off and tossed it to the floor. My heart raced at the river of sweat rushing from between his pecs down that treasure trail of hair that led to his bush. Then he had the shorts off and the jock strap, and they went to the floor on top of the shirt.

"Just so you see what you're missing." Eddie grabbed his dick in his right hand and stretched it out. "You want it, don't you?"

"I do," I said. "Which is why you have to leave."

I turned my back on him and went into the bedroom. I closed the door behind me, wishing that it had a lock—though I wasn't sure if I wanted it to keep Eddie out or keep me in. I kept waiting for Eddie to barge in on me. I knew I wouldn't have the moral character to refuse him if he did.

Fuck you, Eddie Gonzalez.

I heard the shower start, Eddie singing some song in Spanish that I heard in bars sometimes. I stripped down and tossed my sweaty clothes into the laundry hamper, and sat naked and cross-legged on my bed.

The water cut off and Eddie stopped singing. He banged around in the living room, and after a minute or two I heard the front door shut. I went into the bathroom, closing the door behind me, and stepped into the shower, pulling the curtain around the tub, and turned on the water.

For the first couple of minutes of my shower I could barely concentrate. Though Eddie had used my soap and shampoo, the room still smelled of him. After a while either the smell washed away or I got accustomed to it, and I was able to shower and wash my hair. By the time I got out of the shower, he and all his bottles and glasses were gone. Not even a note on the table saying good-bye.

That was when I knew I was right to brush him off. Eddie didn't want the same things from life that I did. I wanted a guy I could count on, a house together, a dog. Maybe even a kid someday. Eddie just wanted the next piece of ass. And even though I was desperate to be that ass for him, I knew I would hate myself afterward.

I had an appointment that afternoon at an upscale Italian restaurant in Aventura, where I was going to train the wait staff on how to recommend and serve my after-dinner tea blends. I went over their menu before I left, figuring out which teas would be a good follow-up to which entrées, and which would complement the dessert menu.

It was good to keep busy. I didn't think about Eddie again until late that evening, when I'd come home from an exhausting couple of hours brewing tea and prepping the staff on techniques and recommendations. The sweaty clothes I'd lent to Eddie were still in a pile on my living room floor, and I picked up the jockstrap and held it to my nose.

Oh, man. In the spring of our senior year, we'd gone running together through the streets of West Philadelphia and into a park called the Woodlands. We'd dart along the curving paths as if we were satyrs in ancient Greece, past an old fieldstone mansion with classical columns and pediment, skirting along the cemetery and its white-washed tombstones.

We'd get back to Eddie's off-campus apartment, strip down and make love while our bodies were slick and fragrant, then shower together in the old-fashioned claw-foot tub with the curtain pulled around us, like we were in our own little world.

I couldn't help myself. I put on the T-shirt and shorts Eddie had worn, still damp and musky, stuck the pouch of the sweaty jockstrap up to my nose and began rubbing my dick through the shorts. I was on the brink of another colossal orgasm when my phone rang with the tone I'd assigned to Parker.

And just like that, my dick wilted and I dropped the jockstrap. What the fuck was I doing?

Chapter 7

To-Do Lists

I knew I'd behaved like a dick. Darren had a boyfriend, and I hadn't respected that. I'd let the little head do the thinking, not the big head. Now, how could I make it right?

Did I even want to? Could I consider running a business with Darren Carter when all I wanted to do was fuck him and make up for all the years we'd been apart? He very clearly wanted nothing to do with me.

When I got back to my apartment, I sat down to look through my spreadsheets again. The numbers told the hard truth: I couldn't finance the expansion I needed without an infusion of cash from Phil Sweet, or someone else.

The problem was that I'd hit up every venture capitalist and angel investor I knew, and Sweet was the only one who'd expressed any interest. Looking at the numbers through his eyes, I could see he was right. My product line wasn't deep enough to succeed on its own.

If I didn't merge operations with Darren, what else could I do? Try and sell the business to some larger company? A liquor manufacturer or distributor? Leverage myself into a job managing the product line for them?

I didn't want to do that. Cockteals was my baby, and I wasn't ready to sell it off for a tiny percentage of its future worth like so much excess inventory.

But could I manage to keep my dick in my pants and work with Darren? Was there some anti-Viagra I could take? Submit myself to electroshock treatments as I looked at naked pictures of him?

The first step had to be an apology. I pulled out my phone and texted Darren. *Loved your tea mixes. We've got to find a way to make this merger work.*

As I waited for the message to be delivered, I wondered if I needed to sell the merger harder. Should I admit that I was sunk without him?

Before I could get too deep into my own head, my phone pinged with an incoming text from Darren. *Loved your drinks too. I agree. How do we work together?*

I reined in my baser impulses. *Let's meet and talk.*

We agreed to meet again the next day. Darren had to train a new barista at a hipster coffee shop in the funky downtown part of Hollywood, and I had a meeting nearby, so I agreed to swing past the coffee shop when I was finished.

A couple of weeks before, I'd gone to a meeting of an entrepreneur's club, where I'd ended up talking to a guy from a brand-new microbrewery. Jean-Pierre was a skinny Haitian-American guy with a hospitality degree from Florida International University in North Miami. He'd been working on the business side of restaurants and bars for a few years and had been hired to open a brewpub on the site of the brewery operation, in an industrial neighborhood of Hallandale, right over the Broward County line.

After we chatted and exchanged business cards, I'd bought a couple of six-packs of their Alligator Amber Ale and begun fiddling with a mix that could jazz up what was basically a pretty bland flavor profile. Once I had something I liked, I pitched Jean-Pierre and he invited me up to meet the father and son who ran the operation.

I brought my traveling liquor bar in case the guys wanted to taste the rest of my line, but I focused on the way they could expand their offerings. "From my research data, I've found that women are more willing to sample beer when it has interesting or unique flavors," I said. "This would be a way for you to serve up a premium product at a slightly higher rate, and attract the lighter drinkers."

"I created that ale," the son said. "It gets great ratings from everybody who tries it."

Both he and his father were heavyset Latin guys who looked like they enjoyed their beer. "I've tried it myself and I think it's great too," I said. "I'm not suggesting you change it—just offer a new twist."

The father nodded, and I asked their permission to step up to a tap and show them what I had. They agreed, and I poured a shot of my custom mix into the bottom of a pilsner glass, then filled the glass from the tap. The herbs in the mix floated up as the beer came down, giving the glass a confetti look. I made a second and handed them over.

The son looked skeptical, but the father picked up the glass and sniffed the bouquet. "Fruity and floral." He sipped it, and I held my breath.

The father loved it, and the son had to admit that it enhanced his brew rather than destroying it. They agreed to take a couple of bottles on consignment, and if it worked out, we'd set up a regular supplier agreement.

Consignment wasn't my favorite business model—I liked to get the money up front, and if I had to take back some half-empty bottles I usually couldn't do anything more than throw the contents away and reuse the bottles.

However, I was pretty confident that if they followed my instructions, and did some promotion, they'd be happy, and I'd be back to sign a real deal.

I drove the couple of miles into Hollywood with a smile on my face and found the coffee shop on a side street. It was a shambles, and I was surprised Darren even bothered with it. It was a high-ceilinged space with what my father would have called "early thrift shop" decor—a couple of mismatched chairs and a couch too low to be comfortable. Too much open space in the center, and along the walls were racks of used clothes and shelves of clay pots and dishes that looked like they'd been made in an elementary school crafts class.

No customers. Darren was behind the counter with a tattooed barista, but he came out as soon as I walked in. "I'm done here," he said. "Let's go somewhere we can talk."

I'd just pumped the meter. "You don't want to stay here?"

He lowered his voice. "You kidding? Look at this place. It's giving me hives, and I'm pretty sure the barista's high and wants to smoke again as soon as I clear out."

There was a Starbucks a few blocks away, and we walked over there. "Why do you bother with a client like this?" I asked.

"It's owned by a recovering heroin addict that Parker used to counsel. I started supplying him as a favor to Parker. Even though it looks dead now, they do a big business after dark."

I refrained from suggesting what they did a business in. "They move merchandise?"

"Enough to make the occasional trip up here worthwhile," he said. "How'd your pitch session go?"

We talked business as we walked. It was a gray, overcast day, damp with a restless breeze that soaked into my exposed skin, and I was glad to get into the welcoming warmth of a working coffee shop. We ordered green tea, and Darren doctored both our cups after we had them.

"Listen, I was out of line yesterday," I said as we sat. "I want to apologize."

"We were both at fault," Darren said. "I think we both got hot-headed and said things we didn't mean."

I'd meant what I said about wanting to fuck him, but I took the higher path and agreed. "The fact is that we need each other," I said. "So either we figure out a way to sail forward together, or we each sink individually."

"Not a happy metaphor, but a true one," Darren said.

"I promise to lay off the sexual innuendo," I said. "Well, I take that back. I promise to do my best to lay off."

"And I promise not to snap back at you."

I held out my hand for Darren to shake. "Deal?"

"Deal."

He shifted around so that we sat side by side and pulled out our laptops, and spent the next hour working on our proposal to Phil Sweet. "What's your demographic?" I asked Darren.

"Anyone who drinks tea."

"Come on, Darren. You know that's too broad. Little old ladies drink tea, but the older demographic is more resistant to change their existing shopping patterns. Right now you're focused on the after-dinner market, right?"

He looked wary but agreed.

"In order to expand beyond that, you need to come up with a profile—someone who is willing to experiment with new flavors, who's willing to spend more for a premium tea product, someone who drinks multiple cups of tea each day."

"I can do some surveys at the restaurants that serve my products. See who's ordering them, and build from that." He looked at me. "What about you? What's your demographic?"

"Hip, urban drinkers who are tired of the same old cocktails," I said right away. "Twenty-one through about forty-five or fifty. Consume five or more mixed drinks per week. Mostly men, though I'm finding through talking to bartenders that women are more willing to order a second drink if it's tea-flavored because there's a slightly lower alcohol content, and they're less likely to get drunk."

Darren looked suitably impressed. "How do you translate that to the retail market?"

"Packaging is going to be key. Men are more likely to shop at a liquor store, while women are more prone to making purchases at grocery stores. Right now my web sales trend about seventy-thirty in favor of men, but I'm adding a new video with a bunch of women drinking in somebody's living room."

By the time we were done, we each had a lot of items on a to-do list, from more market research to packaging to reducing production costs.

"One more thing," Darren said, as we were finishing up. "The name has to change. No more Cockteals."

"What's wrong with my name? It says 'cocktails' and 'tea.'"

"Yeah, it's great for gay bars. And we're expanding the product line, remember? I like '"More than Tea.'"

I blew a raspberry. "Bo-ring."

"Put that on your list. New name that reflects both kinds of products."

I looked at Darren, and he looked back at me, his eyes dancing. Working together was certainly going to be interesting.

Chapter 8

It's Not You

Driving home from Hollywood after meeting with Eddie, I felt excited by my business in a way I hadn't felt for quite a while. Looking at it through Eddie's eyes opened up new possibilities, forced me to face things I'd tried to ignore.

In short, working with him was like old times, only without the sex.

Thinking of sex reminded me of Parker, how I'd ignored his call and how I'd ended things with him so quickly the last time we met. I pulled up at a traffic light on US 1, a fifties-style elementary school on my left and a brand-new high-rise on my right, beside a Spanish Pentecostal church and a café and grocery with signs in Cyrillic.

While I waited for the light to change, I texted Parker an invitation to dinner that evening. I continued to creep down the road, passing a black woman on a bicycle loaded with plastic trash bags and a mechanic in a grease-stained shirt who carried the business section of *El Nuevo Herald*, the Spanish-language edition of the local paper.

As I was getting ready to head east to A1A, Parker accepted my invitation, accompanied by a bunch of vegetable emoticons. The last one was the eggplant, which some people used to mean a penis. But

Parker was a vegetarian and a pretty white-bread guy, so I figured he was using it in a non-ironic way.

I'd gotten accustomed to being creative when I cooked meals for him, so I stopped at a farmer's market and looked for inspiration among the glistening bunches of broccoli, the stacks of sickly-white cauliflower, the five different kinds of winter squash. I settled on a big glossy eggplant that reminded me too much of Eddie's dick, the tall beefy stalk, the way it swelled down to a big round bottom like his hefty balls.

Jesus, I had to get a grip. I bought the eggplant so that I could slice it up when I got home, and I did, trying my best not to think of dicks at all, not Eddie's, not Parker's.

I dipped the slices in beaten egg and flour, sautéed them, layered them into a tray with raw mushrooms and three kinds of cheese. At least Parker wasn't a vegan; he just wouldn't eat anything with eyes.

"Something smells awesome," he said, when he walked in that evening. He'd come straight from work and his tie was crooked, the collar of his white dress shirt unbuttoned. I loved that look on him, the tired but satisfied hero who'd spent his day solving the problems of the world—or at least a couple of clients.

We sat down to dinner, and he told me about his day. "A referral from the community college," he said. "This girl jumped into taking classes without thinking through all her other issues—she has no reliable transportation, a job where they keep changing the hours on her, and on top of that her mother's sick. So of course she's failing everything. She came into my office and started to cry and it took at least ten minutes to get her calmed down."

I shook my head. Parker really was a saint. "What can you do for somebody like that?"

"I got her college advisor on the phone, and he suggested she withdraw from one class and switch to an online section for the other," Parker said. "We drew up a budget for her so she can swap out her crappy car for a better model in a couple of months."

"Wow. That's awesome."

"So is this dinner," he said. "Unfortunately, I can't do anything about the sick mother. I gave her some meditation exercises to do when things get stressful and made a follow-up appointment for next month."

I admired Parker so much for dedicating his life to helping other people. It made the work Eddie, and I were doing seem awfully selfish. I hoped that once I was making a real profit I'd be able to do something good too. Maybe donate product to a homeless shelter or hire ex-cons who needed a fresh start.

"Earth to Darren," Parker said, and I realized I'd zoned out. "How was your day?"

"I met with Eddie Gonzalez again," I said.

"Your ex?"

"Uh-huh. I told you about his business, right? The tea cocktails?"

He nodded.

"We both figured out that Phil Sweet was right. Our product lines aren't strong enough on their own to make a successful consumer business."

"Why do you have to keep pushing?" Parker asked. He sat back from the table, his empty plate in front of him. "You're making a living from what you're doing, right? So keep on doing that."

I shook my head. "I'm not. I've been living off my savings, and besides, I want more than this." I waved my hand around to encompass the tiny crowded apartment. "Don't you?"

"This is why so many people get in trouble," Parker said. "Wanting more than they have, more than they need."

"Come on, Parker. We've talked about the future. Getting a house together, a dog. Maybe even a kid someday. All that takes money. And to get that money, you have to be willing to work hard and do things you don't want to. Like work with an ex-boyfriend."

"You don't have to do that if you don't want to," Parker said.

And right then, I realized that I did want that. I wanted to work with Eddie Gonzalez. And yeah, I wanted to fuck Eddie too. More than once. Which I couldn't do if I was still seeing Parker.

"I think maybe we need to recognize that you and I don't want the same things," I said. "You're content to do your job, to help people, and I think that's awesome. But I want more."

"Is this about your ex?" Parker asked.

"No," I said right off, but backed up. "Well, a little. We had a hot thing for a while, and seeing him again made me realize that you and I don't have that same zing."

"I could try to be more experimental in bed," Parker said. "One of my clients was talking to me about using blindfolds."

"It's not you, it's me," I said, even though I cringed at the cliché.

He pushed his chair back. "I hope that you find what you're looking for, Darren."

And he was gone. Jesus, the guy was kind even when I was dumping him. Had I made a horrible mistake? Eddie was not a guy for the long haul. We'd try and make the business work, but would sex get in the way? Now that I was free, would he even still want me?

I pushed thoughts of Eddie Gonzalez from my mind. I went for a long run along the beach and by the time I got home, I was exhausted. I took a quick shower and fell into bed.

The next morning, though, all those doubts returned, and I immersed myself in my business to push them away.

I ordered most of my tea from my previous employer in Japan, so I had to forecast far enough in advance that I had enough product on hand. It was always a hassle to sit down with my production charts and figure out what was selling, what had to be reordered, and what blends I had to push before the delicate contents were no longer at their best.

Eddie had mentioned that he had a software application that helped him with forecasts. Maybe he could help me automate what was my least favorite part of running my business. I called and he said that he thought it could work, but I'd have to bring my laptop over to his place, and he'd copy the program for me and help me get it set up.

As I rode the bus down to South Beach, I wondered again if I was making a big mistake. Maybe entrepreneurship wasn't for me. Maybe all I wanted was to fuck Eddie again.

Who knew?

When Eddie answered his door, we had a moment of awkwardness. We were old friends, former lovers, future business partners. Were we supposed to shake hands? Hug? Kiss?

Fortunately, Eddie was one of those effusive Latinos, and he enveloped me in a big bear hug. He still smelled the way I'd remembered, a mix of lemon verbena soap and a rum-scented aftershave. After a brief hesitation, I relaxed into his grasp and relished the feel of his strong arms around me.

"I'm glad we figured out how to work together," he said, as we pulled apart. "I realized that I've missed you all these years."

My mouth was dry, but I managed to say that I'd missed him too.

I was surprised at how tiny his apartment was, and yet how Spartan. One wall was lined with plastic bins, each neatly labeled, but that was the only evidence that he ran a thriving business in about six hundred square feet.

A big chunk of that footage was taken up with a king-size bed. Typical Eddie. Live in a tiny studio but keep a huge bed. I tried not to focus on the bed, or what went on in it, and instead sat down at Eddie's kitchen table with him.

Eddie spent a lot of time leaning over me, his shoulder against mine, and it was a struggle to focus on the complicated software and not on the stiffness of my dick in my pants. But once I got the hang of entering data and running analysis, I realized that it could make my chore much easier.

"We're going to need to talk to Phil Sweet and tell him we've reconsidered working together," Eddie said after a while.

"I agree. We should meet with him and see what he wants in a joint proposal."

I had worked with Phil the longest, since our first meeting in Portland a year before, and so I was the one to call his office. "Eddie and I sat down and hashed out our differences," I said, when the receptionist had put me through to him. "We'd like to meet with you again to go over what you'd like to see in a joint proposal."

"You guys have an interesting dynamic," Phil said. "Before we get into the nuts and bolts, I want to see how you could work together. Why don't you both come out on the boat with Margarita and me on Sunday afternoon? I'd like her to meet you, get her opinion on you. We'll cruise around, have some cocktails, and see how things work out."

It wasn't the answer I wanted, but I looked at Eddie, and he nodded. I agreed with Phil and arranged to meet him at the Coconut Grove marina, where he had his yacht docked.

I went back to the program Eddie had given me, figuring out how to generate forecasts, and after a couple of hours I was able to prepare an order for tea from Japan. Eddie was working on a production problem he had, and periodically he'd ask my advice.

This was what I'd hoped for. Eddie and I complemented each other, and despite the five years we'd spent apart, we still knew each other well enough to talk in shortcuts, to make connections and riff off each other's ideas.

Though we talked about a lot of different things, I didn't mention breaking up with Parker. That wasn't germane to the conversation, and I didn't want Eddie to get the idea that I'd done it so I could be with him.

And I didn't know myself.

Chapter 9

Fiesta

You could call it an advantage of moving to Miami, or a disadvantage, but it brought me back to my big Cuban family. I grew up in Westchester, a primarily Hispanic suburb of the city, and now that I was within driving distance, I was required to attend family events, like my *abuela's* eightieth birthday fiesta. So instead of heading out to the bars on Saturday night, I took the causeway to the mainland and then local roads to my parents' house.

They were happy I'd come back to town, but pissed off when I chose to take an apartment instead of moving back in with them. Cuban families are often suffocatingly close, and in many cases kids don't leave home until they marry. My younger sister, Concepcion, was twenty-four, with a college degree and a great job in logistics for one of the cruise lines, and she still lived in the same room she had all her life, though she'd swapped out the Ricky Martin posters I'd secretly coveted as a teenager for some watercolors of the Havana we'd never seen in person.

Our parents had both come to the States as kids, and we'd both been born in Miami. But our grandparents told these romantic stories of starlit nights walking hand-in-hand along the Malecón, the waterfront promenade in La Habana, and Connie had fallen for the romance of it.

Maybe that was why she was still single at twenty-four.

I'd inherited my father's pragmatism. Cuba was an untapped market, and as soon as trade relations relaxed enough, I was going over there to sell product to the high-end hotels and restaurants. I already had a pretty good replica of the classic Cuba Libre, rum and coke, with white tea and a mix of herbs to replace the Coca-Cola.

My parents didn't know I was gay, and I was happy to leave them in the dark. My dad was a macho guy with a mustache, a big belly, and a taste for Cuban cigars. He'd gone to work in construction as soon as he was old enough, and he was now a superintendent for one of the local Latin builders. My mom was a dark-eyed, dark-haired beauty with a pharmacy degree. She worked at a local drugstore and kept the whole family supplied with prescription drugs, aspirin, Band-Aids and other medical paraphernalia. It was a family joke that our medicine cabinet was deep enough to reach all the way to China. I knew that if I came out, my father would bluster about having a son who was a *maricón*, the Cuban slang for faggot, and my mother would obsess about AIDS.

My parents couldn't understand why I'd given up a good job on Wall Street to chase my entrepreneurial dream. Neither of them were tea drinkers—they lived on *cafecito*, the tiny cups of dark, sweet Cuban coffee, and to them tea was a weak substitute. I had tried showing them the way it mixed with rum, but they shrugged and said that it was easier to add *el Coke*.

What are you going to do? They were family.

My mother pulled me aside soon after I arrived. "Ay, Connie is still seeing *ese Americano*," she said, her lip curling in distaste. "See if you can talk some sense into her. You don't know any nice Cuban boys you can introduce her to?"

I couldn't tell my mother that the most serious romance of my life so far had been with an Americano—Darren Carter. She probably wouldn't have minded so much that I was gay, but the boy had to be

Cuban, or at least a Latino, and he had to want a big *familia* with lots of grandchildren for her to spoil.

"I'm not a matchmaker, Mami," I said. "Connie's old enough to pick her own boyfriend."

"But what if he wants to marry her? And take her away from us?"

My parents had both left big families behind on the island, and they were always calling Tía Maria del Carmen in San Cristóbal or sending care packages to cousin Juancho and his family, who lived in a tiny apartment in one of the decaying mansions near the Malecón. It was her greatest regret that Connie and I had to grow up apart from our aunts and uncles and cousins and she was desperate to recreate that experience for her grandchildren.

Her as yet unborn grandchildren, of course. My father often said, *Quiero ser un suegro antes de ser un abuelo*—I want to be a father-in-law before I am a grandfather. Neither of those was going to be a problem in my case.

I followed the soulful voice of Celia Cruz singing to a salsa beat to the backyard, where I found my father tending the barbecue grill, making Cuban-style pork ribs with mojo sauce that was heavy on garlic, pepper, and coriander. He bragged that it was an old family recipe, but it looked suspiciously like one I'd seen one of the Food Network chefs prepare in a video online.

"*Hola, Papi,*" I said. I hugged him, inhaling the scent of bay rum and the cigar he'd been smoking.

"Hola, mi hijo," he replied. "Como esta?"

"*Bien.* Working hard."

That was the way with first-generation Latinos; we spoke to our family and friends in a mix of English and Spanish called Spanglish, and our grandparents always complained about our terrible accents and bad grammar when we spoke Spanish.

"I still don't see why you don't go back to *ese trabajo* on Wall Street. You made *mucho dinero* there, I could brag about you to *mis amigos.*"

It always cracked me up the way he pronounced it "Hole Street," a nickname you might give to a guy who took it up the ass so often there were sidewalks to guide you in.

"Sorry, Papi. My life is about more than something you can brag about over illegal cigars and smuggled rum."

He put his finger up to my lips. "*Cállate la boca*," he said. "*Tu mami* thinks I am smoking *esa mierda* from Honduras."

I helped him turn the ribs, though of course I couldn't do it the way he liked, and he had to reposition the meat on the grill. It reminded me of the way everything in Darren Carter's apartment was arranged so carefully. How I'd wanted to move something around just to irritate him.

My dick swelled uncomfortably at the thought of Darren, and I left my father to go back inside and find my abuela. She was a tiny, wizened woman who dyed her hair jet black and had the smoothest skin of anyone I knew—a lifetime of putting cream on her face every night before bed, she often said.

I kissed her and wished her *feliz cumpleaños,* and she insisted that I sit on one side of her, with Connie on the other as we ate dinner. "Ay, you remind me so much of *mi hermano*, the Eduardo you are named for," she said. "*Muy guapo*."

I'd seen photos of abuela's older brother from back in Cuba. He was very dapper, always photographed in white suits and straw hats. My father had idolized him as a boy, and he'd adopted the bay rum cologne his uncle wore when he got old enough to shave. I used the same. The cologne was in an old-fashioned brown bottle with Spanish writing, made by exiles in Tampa using an old Cuban recipe.

Tío Eduardo had been a political organizer, and he was barely twenty when he was imprisoned in a labor camp by Fidel Castro. His death there had galvanized my grandparents to pack up their family and move to the United States.

My father changed the music on the stereo to some Afro-Cuban jazz, playing softly in the background, and he helped my mother carry the food out. When they put the platters down on the table, he grabbed my mother around the waist and they improvised a couple of dance steps to the music.

They were so easy together, so effortlessly sexy and sweet, and I longed for the same connection. I caught Connie's eye, and I could see she felt the same way.

To accompany my father's ribs, my mother had made my favorite, *Moros y Cristianos*. Instead of serving black beans over a bed of cooked rice as many Cubans did, my mother simmered them both together, with onions, green pepper, garlic, and tomato paste. I'd tried to make it once in Philadelphia to show Darren how awesome Cuban cuisine could be, but my attempt tasted nothing like my mother's.

For a moment I wished he could be there with me to taste it. But that was never going to happen.

It felt good to be back in the bosom of my family, but at the same time I worried about how they would feel if they knew the truth about me. I couldn't see ever bringing Darren, or any other guy, Anglo or Latin, to a family dinner. I worried that my father would never hug me again, that my mother's eyes would fill with sadness.

Maybe if I brought Ricky Martin home, at least Connie would be pleased.

Chapter 10

Shared Past

When Eddie picked me up Sunday morning so that we could talk things over at brunch before going out to meet Phil Sweet, I was surprised that he looked so chipper and well-rested. I'd assumed he was out at the bars the night before, trying to hook up, but he told me he'd gone to his grandmother's birthday party instead.

"I forgot your family lives here," I said as we drove across the causeway to the mainland. It was weird to see all those sailboats and yachts out in Biscayne Bay and realized we were on our way to a boat like one of them. "You see them a lot?"

"Every couple of weeks. My mother breaks out in a rash if she doesn't see me often enough." He looked over at me. "Or at least she says she does. I've never seen evidence."

"I haven't been home in ages," I said. "But my family is nowhere near as close as yours is."

My parents had divorced when I was six. Both had remarried, but my mom and my stepmom didn't get along, so I rarely saw my dad. I had twin stepbrothers nearly ten years younger than I was, and they'd always had that twin thing going on, shutting me out. I'd been glad to escape to college, and I rarely went back to Ohio.

"It's good and it's bad," Eddie said. "Sometimes they get so close they suffocate me. But I don't know what I'd do without them."

"Did you ever come out to them?"

He shook his head. "I told you, my dad's a real macho guy, and he'd never approve. It's easier to keep my romantic life separate."

Romantic. So that was what he called it.

We parked on the edge of downtown Miami near an old-time coffee shop where we could order eggs and home fries without breaking our budgets. With the courthouse and the neighboring offices closed, the streets were almost spookily empty. A homeless guy sat in front of the roll-down metal grate guarding a pawn shop, and he held out his hand to us as we passed, not even bothering to ask for anything, as if he could tell we were only marginally more solvent than he was.

Or maybe he just didn't care.

A waitress in a white uniform with a big fake rose pinned to her breast took our orders. A minute later she was back with big white china cups of boiling water and a pair of no-brand tea bags.

I surreptitiously poured some of one of my mixes into both cups as the water darkened. "What are we drinking?" Eddie asked.

"Elderberry, ginger, and desiccated Meyer lemon peel," I said. "We'll see if it can jazz this up."

"If you can make this generic tea taste good, you're a wizard," Eddie said, as we both swirled the cup so that the flavors would meld. I waited for the mix to cool, but Eddie lifted the cup to his lips and took a sample. He always was willing to go hotter than I was.

"This is delicious," he said. "You're a wizard."

"If ever oh ever a wiz there was, the wizard of tea was one because..." I sang in a low voice, and Eddie laughed.

My omelet was huge, oozing orange cheddar cheese and sautéed mushrooms, with a giant helping of shredded home fries. Eddie had ordered the Eighth Street Special, named after the Cuban neighborhood a few blocks away where his grandparents had first lived when they arrived in the US. Onions, garlic, and a mix of spices rose in a fragrant mist as he dug in.

"I hope you're not planning to kiss anybody after you eat that," I said.

"I could always pucker up to Phil Sweet," he said. His leg touched mine under the table. "Or you."

"Not a chance."

As we ate, we talked about what we needed to know from Phil Sweet. "I'm hoping he can give us sample profit and loss reports from similar businesses," Eddie said. "To see what kind of profit he's hoping we can generate. Help us set revenue targets and market penetration rates."

Penetration.

Focus, Darren.

"I want to know how much he's willing to keep working with us," I said, trying desperately to keep my mind on the topic. "Is he going to be a hands-on investor? Or are we on our own?"

"Hands on," Eddie said, and he smirked.

If we could have bottled the sexual tension rising from both of us that morning, we wouldn't have had to bother pushing tea. I looked down at my plate and realized I'd wolfed down all my food without even realizing it.

Two men at the table beside us were talking in French-accented English about income and spreadsheets. The man facing me was so ugly, I couldn't stop staring at him—a huge square head with grizzled jowls, a protruding lower lip, and unkempt graying hair.

"Am I boring you?" Eddie asked.

"Sorry." I leaned forward. "Look at that guy next to us. Have you ever seen anyone uglier?"

He looked. "You mean uglier than you first thing in the morning?"

I laughed, and kicked him under the table. It felt great to be back with Eddie, but at the same time I worried. What if this reconnection was just a fling, cleaning up some unfinished business from our college days? If we broke up a second time, I'd have more than my heart at risk. My business, my future.

We finished eating, split the check, and drove over to the Coconut Grove marina. It was a gorgeous afternoon, the sky a clear blue with hardly a cloud. Tiny waves made a soft splashing sound against the wooden docks, and every boat looked like it cost more than a college education.

A security guard called Sweet and verified that we were expected, and let us through a locked gate. "Smells like money, doesn't it?" Eddie said to me as we walked down a finger pier toward Sweet's yacht.

Sweet was waiting for us on the dock, in a silk Tommy Bahama Hawaiian-style shirt and Brooks Brothers shorts, with the tiny hanging sheep crest on the pocket. Years in the Ivy League had taught me all those markers of wealth, even if I hadn't noticed the heavy gold bracelet around his wrist, the nine-hundred-dollar loafers on his feet.

He introduced us to his wife Margarita, a beautiful, buxom Latina only a few years older than Eddie and I were, and at least twenty years younger than Sweet. Everything about her from her diamond and gold watch to her Louboutin heels said "trophy wife." She kicked off her heels and stepped barefoot onto the deck, and the flex of her long legs made even a Kinsey six like me take a second look.

You had to call it a yacht, not a boat. A hundred feet, gleaming white, with a narrow prow like the fin of a shark. Everything on board looked like it was the best of the best, from the leather banquette and polished wood table to the painting of a chubby drummer against a small town background that looked suspiciously like an original Fernando Botero.

A light wind blew in off the bay, creating a slight chop in the water, the white froth reminding me of semen. Why was it that every time I was around Eddie Gonzalez I thought about sex?

Sweet went up to the bridge while Eddie helped Margarita cast off the lines. I stayed up by the bow alone and watched as we passed the wooden posts with navigational lights, a cluster of sailboats at anchor in the protected harbor, a couple of guys on personal watercraft zooming around laughing.

We cleared the breakwater, and Sweet called down to me from the bridge to meet him in the salon. Eddie was already there, peering at one of the art works on the wall. "This is it, buddy," he said. "We've got to make this work."

"Agreed."

Sweet came in, and we sat down at the banquette with him as he began teasing out details of the past that Eddie and I shared.

"So you two knew each other at Wharton," Sweet said.

"Eddie went to Wharton. I was in the College," I said. "But yeah, we knew each other."

"How'd you meet?"

I looked at Eddie. Sweet had to know that we were both gay, and it couldn't be a problem for him if we'd come this far. "At a dance sponsored by the gay student group," Eddie said. "Darren's the one who put me onto tea in the first place."

I jumped on that thought. "Eddie was a dyed-in-the-wool coffee drinker. I had to push him to try his first cup of Earl Grey."

"Didn't take to it at first," Eddie said. "I grew up on cafecito, you know. Cuban culture revolves around coffee. Even when my sister and I were babies, we'd get a couple of drops of coffee in our morning milk."

We babbled on for a while about coffee and tea, and finally Sweet said, "So you guys dated?"

I gulped. But one thing I'd learned in the whole venture capital process was that truth had to be the basis of any deal. "Yeah, but when we graduated we went our separate ways. I got a fellowship to study in Japan, and Eddie went to Wall Street."

"And how was that breakup?"

Was the detail of my broken heart relevant to the tea business? I wanted to protest, but I wanted the investment from Sweet more. Eddie and I both spoke at the same time.

"Tough," Eddie said.

"Awful," I said.

We looked at each other. We'd never discussed the way we'd parted—when we met up again we were too consumed with the details of our businesses to hash over old news.

"I'm going to go up and see how Margarita's doing on the bridge," Sweet said, as he stood up. "I need to know that you guys can work together, that there's no bad mojo from the past that's going to jump up and sabotage you."

He walked out of the salon, and Eddie turned to me. "Why do I feel like we're in the middle of an episode of *Dr. Phil* instead of *Shark Tank*?"

"I hear you." I paused, then jumped in. "So it was tough for you after we broke up?"

"It sucked. For the first six months I was in New York, I kept wanting to turn to you all the time, tell you what the job was like, what somebody said, what I saw on the subway. And every time I'd remember that you were on the other side of the world, and it was obvious you didn't want anything more to do with me."

"It wasn't that at all," I protested. "I'd been daydreaming about that year in Japan since I was in high school, and I was committed to it. There was no way we could have kept seeing each other when we were that far apart."

"And you made that decision for us both," Eddie said. "You never heard of Skype? E-mail? How did you know I wouldn't follow you to Japan, get a job with one of the banks there?"

"You don't speak a word of Japanese."

"I knew sayonara when I heard it."

The look in his eyes pierced my heart. I'd been so caught up in my own head back then, determined to take advantage of the fellowship that I'd been offered, that I'd never once considered talking it through with Eddie, seeing how he felt about it, and what we could do to stay together. I'd taken it for a given that ours was a college romance that would not survive graduation.

I'd been wrong, of course. I still lusted for Eddie's hunky body, and there was a hollow space in my chest that made me think my feelings went even deeper than longing for his lips on mine and his dick in my ass. Did he feel the same way?

"I'm sorry," I said. "I was a selfish prick. I should have talked to you about Japan. But I thought you were so determined to go to Wall Street that nothing I could say would change your mind."

"Not even if I'd told you that I loved you?"

Crap. The *L* word. We'd never said it to each other. "Would you have said it?"

"You never gave me the chance."

I sighed. "Oh, Eddie. What are we going to do?"

"Convince Sweet that we can work together so he'll give us the money. Can you do that? Work with me?"

"Of course. You know me better than anyone, even after all these years. Our skill sets complement each other—you know the business terms, and I can leverage my palate, my Japanese skills, and my tea knowledge."

"I know a fair bit about tea myself," Eddie grumbled.

"You know what I mean. I've always been more creative than you."

"Not in bed."

My dick twitched. "Is that what we have to do in order to work together? Go to bed? You want to ask Sweet? I'm sure he's got a spare cabin here. We could go to it right now, get it out of the way."

"Jesus, Darren, where'd this asshole side of you come from?"

I had a sudden insight. "That's what this is all about," I said. "This whole business deal. You're pissed that I left you to go Japan, and you want to get back at me. You've know about my business all along, haven't you? You deliberately started a company to screw me over."

Eddie shook his head. "You always had an ego, buddy, but I never realized it was so delusional. Yeah, I've devoted the last five years of my life to building a business that I could use to get some twisted revenge on you."

When he said it, I realized how stupid an idea it was, and I felt deflated. I was a moron, wasn't I? How could I expect to run a successful business if I couldn't keep hold of my emotions. I felt tears begin to prick at my eyes, and I gulped.

Darren slid over on the banquette and put his arm around my shoulders. "Don't cry, Darren, please. I'm sorry."

"No, I'm the one who's sorry. It's not all about me. You have your own life and your own goals, and it's downright stupid of me to think you did everything because of me."

"Well, not everything," Eddie said. "I did like the idea of a tea business because it reminded me of you, and the great times we had in your apartment, drinking tea."

"And afterward," I said, and I smiled.

He nodded. "And afterward." He paused for a moment. "So what do you think? Can we do this?"

I took a deep breath. "We can." I reached out to shake his hand, and at that moment Sweet came back into the salon.

"Good," he said. "Now let's talk numbers."

Chapter 11

Charity Case

The night after our cruise with Phil and Margarita Sweet, I drove up to Darren's to hash out some more details. "Is it me, or is Phil not so sweet anymore?" I asked, as he let me into his crowded little apartment. "Did you see that last e-mail he sent, about profit margins? That he wants to insert a clause into our agreement that if we don't make certain targets within the first year, he can back out?"

"Yeah, that freaked me out when I read it. But I figured that was just business, right?"

I followed him to his kitchen table and set my laptop on it. "Yeah, it's business. But I thought Phil was, you know, a nicer guy."

"Yeah, nice is what got him that hundred-foot yacht and the trophy wife," Darren said.

Once we got down to the mechanics of working together the day before, Sweet had switched gears. He was no longer the friendly mentor both Darren and I had experienced. He was much more a hard-nosed businessman.

The e-mails he'd begun sending the night before were very direct —he "needed" certain things from us. We "had" to fulfill certain obligations. I started to feel overwhelmed, doubting that this was the right move.

"It's getting pretty scary," Darren said, as he sat across from me. "You're the numbers guy. Do you think we can do everything he wants?"

"I don't know. I took a big leap when I quit my job and moved back here to start Cockteals, but now I'm freaking out all over again."

Darren leaned back in his chair. "What made you come back to Miami?" he asked. "Because of your parents?"

"A little. They'd been complaining that they never saw me, that I was always so busy at work. And when I started running the numbers for the business, I realized that there was no way I could afford to live in the city while I was developing things. I came home for a vacation and went around to a couple of bars and restaurants, and I checked out the deals on Airbnb and found an apartment that was way cheaper than what I was paying in Brooklyn. So it all came together."

I looked at him. "What about you? Why Miami?"

"Phil said he could help me a lot more if I was closer to him. And I had nothing keeping me in Portland."

"You weren't seeing anyone?"

The kettle boiled, and Darren got up to make us tea. Or perhaps so that he wouldn't have to look at me.

"I was," he said. "A guy I met at the museum where I was working. Akira."

"Japanese?"

Darren nodded. "Born in Japan, but raised in Sacramento. He used to jokingly refer to himself as a banana—yellow on the outside, but white on the inside."

I hesitated to make a judgment, but I was curious. "Sounds like he wasn't a very happy guy."

"He wasn't. Which was the big reason why we broke up."

He poured some tea and herbs into his infuser and turned back to me.

"It took me a while to realize that he was a very negative guy by temperament. Not only not supportive of my business, but he was sure that I was going to fail and couldn't understand why I'd take such a big risk."

"I'm not sure I understand why either of us did this," I said, as Darren poured tea for both of us in stoneware mugs. "I mean, I had a good job, lots of disposable income, but I felt restless. And when I got the idea for Cockteals, it seemed right."

Darren sat down again. "I didn't have a great job like you did, and I was making barely enough to get by. I was pretty miserable, feeling sorry for myself, and Akira wasn't helping. Then my grandmother died, and surprisingly she left each of her grandkids a chunk of change. I'd never even known she had money, she lived so frugally."

"That's awesome."

"Yeah, but I felt like that money came with responsibility. I wasn't going to end up like her, bitter and cranky and miserly. So I bit the bullet and decided to remake my life."

I lifted the mug and sniffed. "Coconut and blueberry?"

"With green tea," he said.

I lifted my mug to click against his. "To both of us remaking our lives."

Over the next couple of days, documents went back and forth as we figured out the ownership structure of the new operation and went about setting up business licenses, bank accounts, and so on.

Darren and I both still had to manage our ongoing companies while we worked out the terms of the agreement with Phil Sweet. I had to go out to Hialeah to the bottling facility that made and packaged my simple syrups one day to do some quality testing, and I invited Darren to go with me.

The manager of the operation was a heavyset Latino named Jesus, and he spoke rapid Spanish with a South American accent. I answered him in the Spanglish I used with my parents—though I'd grown up in Miami, in a Spanish-speaking household, I was nowhere near as fluent as I could be.

I introduced Darren in English, and when Jesus said he was pleased to meet Darren, I could hear his heavy accent and realize why he'd always spoken Spanish. He tried to speak English as we walked over to the production line, but quickly he lapsed back into Spanish.

The factory floor was noisy, with the *rat-tat-tat* of the capping machine and the *whoosh* of liquid spurting out of nozzles and into bottles. The factory also prepared private label juices for one of the Latin groceries, and the air was filled with the smells of my childhood —tart orange, sweet guava, and the pumpkin-sweet potato scent of *mamey sapote*, my dad's favorite drink.

We tasted a couple of random samples of different mixes, and everything looked good. I picked up a finished bottle and made sure the label was straight. Every now and then I'd translate something for Darren, but he seemed to understand most of what was going on, especially since Jesus peppered his speech with English words for the machinery, like *el* bottle cleaner and *los* labeling machines.

I was surprised when, as we left, Darren thanked Jesus for his time in what sounded like pretty decent Spanish. "I didn't realize you speak Spanish," I said as we walked out.

"I don't. But I figure if I'm going to stay in Miami, I ought to learn a few useful words and phrases, so I've been fiddling with one of those online language tutors. "*Buenos dias, senorita. Tu cochinillo es muy bonito.*"

I laughed. "How often do you get to tell a girl that her piglet is pretty?"

"I haven't used it yet," Darren said. "But it's more about getting your tongue around the words and the accent, isn't it?"

I had a momentary memory of the way Darren had used his tongue on me in the past, and my dick began to stiffen. "If you say so," I said. "I'd focus more on stuff like please keep the noise down. *Por favor, mantenga el ruido abajo.*"

He repeated the phrase a couple of times until he had it right, and it was sweet to see him trying so hard.

That night, my Colombian hookup Luis texted me again. I didn't want to see him, but I was horny after spending so much time around Darren so I gave in, and told him to come over to my apartment.

You'd think my dick would have popped up the moment Luis came in the door and deep-kissed me, but it wasn't cooperating. All I could focus on was the smell of sweat mixed with a sickly sweet cologne he'd obviously sprayed on before arriving. His body was lumpy where I wanted him to be sleek, like Darren, and it wasn't until he began pinching and twisting my nipples that my dick finally got with the program.

He got down on his knees in front of me, unhooked my belt and my pants, and pulled my dick out through the slit in my boxers. I looked down at his greasy curls and thought, I don't want this. I want Darren, goddammit.

And just like that, my dick deflated.

"What's the matter, mi amor?" Luis looked up at me.

I backed away, stood up, and zipped up. "I'm sorry. This isn't working for me. I'll blow you if you want, because you came all the way over here."

"I am not some *caso de caridad*," he said angrily. He stood up and sneered at me. "There are plenty more guys better looking than you."

He turned around and stalked out of the apartment. Of course, as soon as he was gone, my dick popped up as I thought about Darren and how much I wanted him there. I shucked my clothes and lay down on my bed, where I closed my eyes, thought of Darren, and started rubbing one out.

I imagined that was his head beneath me instead of Luis's, that it was his tongue tangoing with mine, that it was his sweet ass opening like the slow-motion blossoming of a rose as the mushroom head of my dick nosed its way in.

I shot a gusher of cum that sprayed up onto my chest. I was so fucked. Maybe Luis wasn't a charity case, but I sure was.

Chapter 12

Still Got It

Eddie and I spoke every day, sometimes multiple times a day. Wednesday we met at a bank in Miami Beach to open our business account. I rode the bus down to Lincoln Road with a skinny man with disheveled hair who spoke out loud the whole way —and I was pretty sure he had no Bluetooth earpiece. Probably no cell phone either.

I got off at the corner of Lincoln Road and Alton Road by the big parking garage that always looked unfinished because of its rough walls and the way it appeared from the outside like you could drive right off the edge of any level and go sailing out over the crowds of burger aficionados and coffee snobs who clustered around the stores at the ground level.

Eddie was waiting for me outside the bank. I couldn't help but notice how good he looked, in a short-sleeved plaid shirt that hugged the contours of his chest, and low-hanging slacks that accentuated his narrow waist.

The assistant manager who helped us was a motherly woman, with dyed red hair and rhinestone-framed reading glasses on a chain around her neck. "You make a very cute couple," she said as she handed us documents to sign. "I hope your business works out."

"We're not a couple," Eddie said. "I mean, we're friends and we used to..." He trailed off.

"TMI," I said to him, then turned back to the manager, whose name was Avis. "We've known each other a long time, but right now we're just business partners."

We were supposed to be concentrating on the forms we had to sign, but I kept sliding looks at Eddie. Was Avis picking up on some vibe between us? Did Eddie want to fuck? My dick was telling me that I sure did, that I wouldn't have minded if he'd pushed me down on Avis's desk and fucked my ass like he had back when we were in college.

My dick was uncomfortably hard, squashed into my pants, and I felt the precum wetting my boxers. I couldn't even adjust myself without revealing to Eddie what I was feeling so I suffered and signed the forms where I was supposed to.

The bank was in a repurposed car dealership, with high ceilings that made the cubicle walls of the management staff look tiny. The tellers were behind floor-to-ceiling glass walls like they needed to be hermetically sealed in. Avis took some cash from us to kick off the account and disappeared through a coded entrance to finish the transaction.

"It's really happening," I said. "As soon as we get the account number to Phil, he promised to deposit some operating capital for us. And we're off to the races."

"When I was in a management class one semester, my professor used to complain that everybody wanted to be on the finance side of the business world," Eddie said. "We wanted to float bonds for the construction of a race track, to syndicate shares in a race horse. Nobody wanted to be the horse."

"Which means?"

"That we're the horses now, baby. We're the ones who make the track work."

"I feel more like the guy who follows the horses around scooping up the manure," I said.

Eddie laughed as Avis returned. "Here's your deposit slip and your package of starter checks. Good luck!"

We thanked her and walked out. "We should celebrate," I said.

"Not until we see the money come in," Eddie said. "I like Phil a lot, and he's been a good guy, but I don't trust anybody until I see the green of their money."

"How about me?"

"You're different," Eddie said. "You've got skin in the game. If this business goes belly up, we both lose everything. Phil? He walks away and takes a tax write-off."

Eddie was starting to remind me of Akira and his negativity, and that was a real mood killer. "I've got some work to do," I said. "You want to hit a coffee shop and get some Wi-Fi?"

"Sure."

We walked out of the bank and headed down Lincoln Road, empty storefronts sprinkled between stores selling sunglasses, watches, and expensive face creams. An incongruous German hofbrau with blue and white check tablecloths sat right beside a Cuban cigar and mojito bar.

A beefy guy in a green uniform for a company that serviced draft beer systems passed us, pushing a hand truck, and my mouth went dry as I imagined Eddie in a uniform like that, hugging his muscles like a second skin.

We settled at a Starbucks a few blocks down, a few doors down from a construction site that promised forthcoming "flagship retail" and a rooftop café from an out-of-town chef with a couple of Michelin stars under his toque.

While Eddie went to order our tea and my laptop was booting up and connecting to the Internet, I looked outside at the passing parade. A couple of teenage girls wearing wooly hats with rabbit ears and T-shirts advertising a website where you could post pictures of whatever you liked, secure in the knowledge that they'd disappear after a few minutes instead of hanging around to haunt you when you applied for a job.

I dosed the tall clear cups of tea with some of my herb and spice mix, and Eddie e-mailed the bank information to Phil Sweet. We both settled down to handle ongoing business, and a couple of hours passed. I realized my stomach was grumbling and the sun was starting to set over Lincoln Road. "Want to get some dinner?"

"We could do takeout and go back to my apartment," Eddie said. "I've still got more work to do."

"Yeah, I do too." We packed up and headed toward his place.

We picked up a whole rotisserie chicken from the postmodern Publix with the ramped escalator for shopping carts, pairing it up with a premade salad and a side of creamed spinach.

We ate at his kitchen table, and I was uncomfortably aware of how close his bed was, and how easy it would be for the two of us to simply move over there. Had his tastes changed in the last five years? I knew he still wore the same cologne, ate the same food, laughed the same way. Would he still fuck the way we had in college?

I shifted my legs so that my dick wasn't trapped in my pants again, the way it had been at the bank. Jesus, I was horny. I might have to resort to one of those online hook-up apps to work things out.

When we finished eating, we went back to work, and suddenly Eddie said, "Holy shit."

"What?"

He swiveled his laptop so I could see the screen. The joint account we'd opened that day had a pending transfer of twenty-five thousand dollars.

I swallowed hard. "It's happening."

"Damn right it is." Eddie grabbed his phone and hit a couple of buttons and suddenly Latin music was playing through speakers over his bed. He jumped up and grabbed my hand. "Come on, let's dance."

"Eddie," I protested. "You know I can't dance the way you do."

"Let's see if you remember anything I taught you." He stepped back and began swiveling his hips in a motion that made my mouth water. "Come on, loosen up those Americano muscles."

I tried to ape his movements.

"That's it, relax your back, feel the rhythm." He took my hand and twirled me around and pulled me close to him, swaying so that his dick pressed against my ass. It felt like an iron rod poking against me, and I remembered all those times we'd danced together in college, how we'd moved so sinuously together across the floor and into bed.

He pushed me away and twirled me again, and this time when I came back to him we were face-to-face. Fuck it. I leaned forward and kissed him.

For a moment I worried I'd misinterpreted the signs, that I'd made a huge mistake. Then he kissed me back.

We swayed together as the music changed to a slower beat, kissing each other deeply, grinding our dicks against each other, and I felt overwhelmed by sensuality. I loved the way Eddie's five-o'clock shadow felt against my cheek, the way his heartbeat pulsed against his chest, the glazed look of lust in his eyes.

The song ended, and Eddie stepped back. "You don't want to do this," he said. "You have a boyfriend, remember?"

"Not anymore," I said. "I broke up with him last week. Because I had to admit that what I felt for you was way more than I felt for him."

I swallowed hard. "Oh, Eddie," I said, and we were back in each other's arms again. I reached around behind him and pulled the tails of his plaid shirt out of his slacks. I stuck my hands up beneath the fabric and felt the silky hairs of his back. His skin was hot under my fingers.

I cursed that I'd worn a polo shirt that day—I had to back away from him to pull it over my head. As I did, he shucked his shirt and then unbuckled his belt and dropped his pants. "Still wearing those same wild boxers," I said.

Back in college, Eddie had worn boxer shorts in tropical prints—

parrots perched in palm trees, monkeys frolicking in the jungle, pirate ships and mermaids. The ones he'd worn that day were similar, a mixture of beer mugs and wine glasses. I knew that what was inside was enough to intoxicate me, though.

"And you? Still wearing those weird Japanese undies?" he asked.

"Why don't you open my pants and see?"

I'd discovered *fundoshi* when I was studying Japanese culture at Penn. They were the traditional underwear for Japanese men way back when, a white cotton loincloth sometimes gathered into a pouch. It was mostly ceremonial in Japan by then, but they were sexy, and I ordered mine from an online store in Japan. Most of mine were plain white, but for some reason I'd worn a red one that morning. Had I known that Eddie would end up seeing it?

He whistled. "Man, that is sexy." He ran his hand over my abs, and I was proud that I'd kept my stomach reasonably flat. "Almost a shame to pull your dick out of them." He grinned devilishly. "But I'm going to."

He dropped to his knees and began to lick my stiff dick through the cotton pouch. I groaned with pleasure, and a moment later he'd shifted fabric so that my dick popped out the side. He took me in his mouth and began sucking with a slow, steady pressure.

I closed my eyes and gave into the sensation. But I realized that I wanted to see Eddie blow me, see his red lips around my dick, the tiny trickle of sweat down the side of his face.

It was all too much, too fast. I backed away and tugged on his shoulders. He stood up and kissed me again, and his dick popped out of the slit in his boxers to rub against mine. He grabbed his phone, and hit a couple of keys, and the music started again. He wrapped his arms around me and pulled me close.

The song was fast and happy, and it mirrored how I felt. We rubbed against each other, backed off and twirled, pulled close. "I haven't heard this before," I said, trying to slow down so that I wouldn't erupt at any second. "Who's playing?"

"A Colombian band," he said. "Puerto Candelaria. They say they're the music of Macondo."

The name rang a bell, but I couldn't place it.

"Gabriel Garcia Marquez, *One Hundred Years of Solitude*," he said. "Macondo is the town in the book. The band plays happy music."

"I'm feeling pretty happy myself right now."

He grabbed my stiff dick in his hand. "I can tell."

"Will you fuck me, Eddie? Like you used to do?"

"With great pleasure." He kissed me and gently pushed me away, toward his bed.

I tugged down the fundoshi and left it on the floor beside the rest of my clothes, then sprawled on my back on Eddie's bed, my legs spread and my ass gaping open. I was so hot for Eddie I could barely breathe.

He didn't make me wait. In only a minute he had shucked his boxers and had a condom on his dick, a bottle of lube in his hand. He squirted some on his index finger and began to stroke my hole. The sensations raged through my body like a wildfire. "You're tormenting me," I panted. "I need you inside me. Now."

"You always were a pushy bottom," Eddie said.

"And you always obliged."

"So basically nothing's changed," he said, as he climbed up onto the bed between my legs and guided his dick into me. He'd done a good job of opening me up, so I felt only a brief starburst of pain, and he was inside me, filling me up in the way no one had been able to do since. We moved in synch, him thrusting in and me pushing forward to meet him, and his dick banged my prostate and sent waves of pleasure through my body.

He balanced on one hand and used the other to fist my dick. I loved the sensation of his damp palm against the base of my dick, the way he teased the sensitive spot beneath my slit because he knew it drove me wild. Sweat pooled under my arms, dripped down my neck. I smelled Eddie's bay rum cologne, tasted the flavor of the chicken on his lips. I wanted to eat him up, swallow him inside me so that I would never miss him again.

"You feeling me, baby?" he asked, as he slammed into me and my ass muscles contracted around him. "You miss your papi all these years?"

"Wait," I panted. "Wait until I come. Then I'll know."

He lifted back his head and roared with laughter. "My sweet *hombrecito*," he said. "Oh God, I've missed you."

"Not as much as I missed you," I said. He stabbed at my prostate and my back arched and I whimpered with pleasure as my orgasm rose from deep in my balls and swirled through my body like a rising wave in a Hokusai print.

My pleasure kicked his over the edge, and he began heaving and moaning in meaningless Spanish syllables. Suddenly he was spurting inside me, his pleasure amplifying my own.

"We've still got it, baby," he said, when he pulled out and collapsed beside me.

"We do. The only question is can we keep doing this and run a business together too?"

Chapter 13

Honeybush

I woke up Thursday morning with Darren in my bed, and for a moment it was as if the last five years hadn't happened, and we were still together in Philadelphia.

He turned to face me and grinned, and I remembered the night before. I must not have looked as happy as he did, because he asked if I had a hangover.

"Nope. I'm good. You?"

"Better than good. Great." He sat up beside me. "And you? Okay with what happened?"

I leaned over and kissed him lightly on the lips. "Better than okay."

He went into the shower while I checked my e-mail on my iPad. The brew pub in Hallandale was doing a bang-up business in tea-beer mixes and needed more stock. A restaurant on Alton Road, though, was going out of business, and if I wanted my stock back, I had to get there that morning before the creditors came in.

When Darren got out of the shower, I hurried in, and we split up with a plan to reconnect late that afternoon at his place.

It was one of those days when I couldn't seem to get ahead, jumping from one problem to the next. Was I ever going to be able to get past the hands-on part of the business? Working with Darren, could we split up the deliveries and the customer service, or would things only get more complicated once we had to deal with distributors and grocery and liquor stores?

It didn't occur to me that working with Darren would be a problem now that we were lovers again until I got to a bar on South Beach where I'd had a couple of romps with the manager. Keshaun was a tall, light-skinned black guy with a shaved head, a goatee, and intriguing tattoos on his chest and arms. People often mistook him for one of the retired players from the Miami Heat, and when asked, he always politely signed the player's autograph.

We sat down at a table in the back of the bar to go over accounts, and when we were finished, he stretched one of his long legs out to rest against mine. "Haven't seen you for a while, bro," he said. "What have you been up to?"

"Trying to launch a retail business," I said. "Selling cocktail mixes to groceries and liquor stores. I have a partner who's doing the same thing, only with custom tea blends."

"All work and no play makes Eddie a dull boy," he said, grinning at me. "Want to play around tonight?"

My dick jumped. Keshaun was a fun lover, athletic and innovative, with a long slim dick that curved slightly at the end, the better to tease a prostate with. And even though Darren and I hadn't talked about exclusivity, I knew from the past that he believed in monogamy, and I couldn't cheat on him the very next day after we'd reunited.

Or ever, I thought with a jolt. Was I ready to settle down to the same dick and ass for the rest of my life? Being with Darren made me feel that way, like a part of me had gotten broken off five years before when he left for Japan. And only now that he was back in my life did all the pieces fit together again.

"Sorry, I'm seeing someone," I said to Keshaun. "My business partner. Also my ex from years ago."

"That's cool." Keshaun rubbed his leg against mine. "Just don't forget me if you end up on the market again."

I gulped. "I'll keep that in mind."

When I arrived at Darren's apartment late in the afternoon, I discovered that his day had been no better than mine. "I'm going to have to reformulate my honeybush tea. The leaves I've been using are only grown in small areas of South Africa, and due to low rainfall in the mountains, the last harvest was dismal. Consequently, the price is skyrocketing."

"Can you use a different species?" I asked.

"I can, but each one has a slightly different flavor profile, and I'm going to have to tinker with the blends."

He stood up and opened the tall cabinet in his kitchen that he'd outfitted with shelves to store all his herbs and teas. "I don't even have enough on hand to finish my current orders. Crap and double crap."

"There must be more than one supplier out there," I said. "Send me the information and I'll look around for you."

He went back to his computer and e-mailed me the Latin name, *Cyclopia intermedia*, and while I went shopping for product he started pulling out packets of other varieties.

The next hour, his apartment was filled with the scent of honey as he brewed up a couple of different varieties for us to taste. Eventually I found a supplier who could ship him enough of the original tea to fill his orders, though at a slightly higher price than he'd been paying.

"There goes my profit margin," he grumbled. "But thanks. I appreciate the help."

He leaned down and kissed me on the lips, and his breath smelled of the honeybush tea. I liked that.

"You're my honeybush," I said, smiling. "Sweet, with a hint of spice."

"And sexy too?"

"Of course."

That led to the inevitable cuddling, and it was only when my stomach grumbled loudly that we broke apart. "Guess I ought to feed you," Darren said. "Something more nutritious than my dick."

He backed away.

"I looked it up once. Only like five percent of semen is sperm, and the rest is like over two hundred separate proteins."

"You're a stud, Eddie," Darren said. "And so am I. But neither of us is going to survive on a teaspoon or two of semen a day, even if it's packed with calories. How do you feel about pasta?"

"If you fix it, I'm sure it will be superb."

"Right. There's a head of garlic in the fridge. Can you dice it up while I get everything else ready?"

We worked easily together, moving around Darren's tiny kitchen as I chopped the garlic and a chunk of pancetta. I sautéed the ham as he boiled the pasta, and by the time I'd added the garlic to the pan, the pasta was ready, and I stepped away to watch him mix the pasta into the garlic-pancetta mixture, then beat eggs and parmesan cheese together.

"This is where it gets tricky," Darren said, as he poured the contents of the frying pan into the bowl. "You don't want the eggs to scramble, which is why you do this off the heat."

I watched as he added some of the pasta water to thin out the sauce. "There are bowls in that cabinet," he said, and I set the table. We sat down to eat a minute or two later, and the pasta was amazing. "I don't remember you cooking much in college," I said.

"I didn't know how. It wasn't until I moved to Portland that I realized I'd better learn to fix meals or else live on fast food and get fat."

"No danger of that," I said. "You're still as skinny as you were at Penn."

"Not really. And I have to work at it now. Have to stay slim for my sexy boyfriend."

"That's what we are again," I said. "Weird, isn't it? After all this time?"

"Weird but inevitable, don't you think? I never got over you. Did you get over me?"

I thought about it before I spoke. "I think maybe I kept to one-night stands because you spoiled me for romance," I said finally. "I justified it by saying that I was young and naive back then, but I think we didn't realize what we had was so special."

"You're a sweetheart," Darren said, and he leaned over and kissed me, the garlic and ham on his breath. I kissed him back, and we left the dirty dishes on the table and moved into the bedroom.

We collapsed onto his bed together, kissing and rubbing against each other and after a couple of minutes I said, "Why are we still wearing clothes?"

"Because you're such a sexy stud that I can't stop kissing you long enough to strip," Darren said.

I snorted and pulled away. It didn't take long until we were both naked and back in that same embrace. This time, though, I wrapped my hand around both our dicks and began to jerk us slowly, feeling the exquisite torture of my rough skin against one side of my dick, and the smooth hardness of Darren's dick on the other.

He groaned. "You make me crazy."

"I can do more than that," I said. I scooted around so that my mouth was at his dick and took him in. He did the same for me. I grabbed the smooth round globes of his ass and buried my face in his pubic hair, nearly choking myself, but I didn't care. I wanted Darren's dick and his cum and nothing was going to stop me.

It was hard to concentrate, though, when his velvet tongue was caressing my dick and pulling me closer and closer to orgasm. My body tingled, and occasionally I had to pull off Darren's dick to take big gulps of air. I came first, shooting off down his throat as my body writhed in the throes of my orgasm. I kept on sucking Darren with the desperation of a drowning man, and he came a moment later, his body stiffening under me as he made little mewling sounds.

I looked up at him and smiled. "My honeybush," I said. "I love the taste of your tea."

He giggled. "You are a goofball." His eyes were glazed with something that looked an awful lot like love, and I hoped he saw the same thing in mine.

Chapter 14

Now and Forever

Eddie and I met with Phil Sweet Friday afternoon to go over all the progress we'd made. "A company I've invested in sells gourmet potato chips, which are produced at a manufacturing plant in Ohio that might also be able to take on your products," he said. "I think you guys ought to fly up there and talk to them."

"Where in Ohio?" Darren asked.

"Town called Barberton, outside Akron. Otherwise known as the middle of nowhere."

"I know it," Darren said. "I grew up in January River. Not far from there."

"I've never been there myself," Sweet said. "But they do a good job with chips. Any reason why you can't go up there next week?"

Eddie and I looked at each other, and both of us shrugged. Phil made a call and arranged for us to get a tour of the facility the following Friday.

Sweet was okay with most of our projections but was worried about some of the costs of producing my mixes. "You've got too many ingredients in some of these," he grumbled. "It's going to be complicated to produce, and if any one of these prices goes up, you could lose your profit margin. You need to work on reformulating."

I opened my mouth to protest, but I caught Eddie's eye. Instead, I swallowed my argument and said, "I'll see what I can do."

"Good man," Sweet said. A few minutes later his secretary announced his next meeting, and he shooed us out.

As we walked back to Eddie's apartment, I was angry. "Why did he pick on me?" I asked. "You could have the same problem with ingredients in your simple syrups. One price goes up and you're toast."

"Yeah, but the most complicated of my syrups has five ingredients. That complexion tea of yours has what, twelve? What the hell is bilberry, anyway? I see you have it in a couple of mixes."

I was ready to argue about the need for all those ingredients, but Eddie diverted me by asking about bilberry. "European version of blueberries," I said. "They're tough to cultivate so mostly they're harvested in the wild in places like Ireland and Finland."

"Which could cause supply problems," Eddie said. "Suppose global warming hits Finland and the reindeer move south and eat all the wild bilberries. You're screwed then."

I wanted to protest that reindeer and global warming had nothing to do with bilberries, but Eddie had a point. "I'll see if I can substitute blueberry extract," I said.

By the time we reached Eddie's place, I was intrigued by the possibility of swapping bilberries, which I had to admit were tougher to source and more expensive, for the more reliably available blueberries. It was one thing to produce a couple of pounds of tea mix every few weeks for delivery to restaurants, and quite another to mass produce.

While I started reviewing the ingredient lists for the mixes we had decided to produce, Eddie opened up his laptop. A few minutes later he said, "I can get us a flight to Akron on Thursday afternoon. Price goes way down if we stay over Saturday night. That okay with you?"

"A weekend with you in Ohio in January? It's like a dream come true," I said. "You know the weather's probably going to be crap? Bitter cold, sleet, snow, the whole winter wonderland."

"We'll both have to suck it up," Eddie said. "If I get cold, you'll have to keep me warm."

He went through Airbnb and found us a room at a small family-owned motel on the outskirts of Barberton. We reorganized our calendars so that we could leave town, and worked our way through dinner, stopping only for a brief cuddle before falling asleep.

The next week flew by. We were both working nonstop, putting out fires, developing new contacts, and also working on the details of the new business.

We decided to use my place as our office, both as a laboratory for developing and tasting flavors, and for ironing out business details, and we kept Eddie's tiny studio as our haven, where we could chill out by listening to music, dancing, and of course having sex. I was glad he'd chosen an apartment that came with a king-size mattress and frame, which he'd begun calling our conjugal bed.

Monday morning, we did a review of each other's products to see if we could make any suggestions. I told him that his rose pomegranate mar-tea-ni got cloyingly sweet the more you drank of it, and I suggested that he might add a pinch of lemon zest to the mix to sharpen the flavor. "You want people to drink more than one, after all," I said.

"You think? Usually women prefer sweet drinks."

"Some do, of course. But you can get too sweet."

He puckered up and gave me an air kiss. "You think so?"

I kicked him lightly. "Focus. I think this drink can be."

"Fine. Mix something up for me."

I went to the counter and grated a bit of lemon zest, then stirred it into the drink I'd been tasting. "Yeah, I like this," I said.

"I like looking at your ass."

"Eddie." I handed him the glass. "What do you think?"

He inhaled it, sipped it, let the liquid swirl around. "Yeah, I think you're right."

I didn't have anything else to suggest, so we moved on to my mixes. "Why do you have to use real cinnamon in your blends?" Eddie asked me. "Cassia is much cheaper. I've seen some vendor prices up to ten times more than cassia."

"Cassia doesn't have the same richness of flavor," I said. "They both come from the bark of evergreen trees. True cinnamon comes from Sri Lanka, and it's lighter than cassia, which comes from Indonesia. And cassia is stronger and hotter, while Ceylon cinnamon is lighter and brighter. More of a taste of cloves, and more citrusy."

"Prove it to me. Let's do a test."

"I don't even have any cassia," I grumbled. "I don't like it."

"It's not always all about you," Eddie said. "When I go out to pick up dinner, I'll get some from the grocery."

"You won't be able to tell," I said. "Most commercially packaged cinnamon doesn't indicate what species of tree it comes from."

"It makes the most sense they'd use the cheaper product, right?"

I agreed that was probably true. "Make sure to get the store brand," I said. When he returned later that afternoon, I made us a quick dinner, and we tested different blends with cassia and with cinnamon. I found that if I cut back the amount of cassia a bit, I was able to wipe out the sharpness and leave the spicy flavor.

"You're right," I said when we finished the taste test. "Again. I hate it when that happens."

"Get used to it, bud," he said. "If we're going to be together for the long haul, you'll find I'm right most of the time."

"And arrogant," I said. I leaned over and kissed him. "Fortunately I find that kind of behavior sexy."

He kissed me back, then wrapped his arms around me and pulled me close. "You do, don't you?" he said. "You like me to go all alpha on you."

I smirked. "Yeah, I love it when you beat your hairy chest and make those monkey noises."

He pounded his chest lightly with his fists and hooted. "Me big alpha gorilla. Want you to be my mate."

I laughed, but my dick began to unfurl in my pants. "Will you fuck my ass?" I said into his ear, licking around the edge. "Will you take that big dick of yours and stick it up my hole and bang it against my prostate until I come from feeling you inside me?"

Eddie groaned. "You make me so horny," he said. "Man, my dick is like iron already."

I stood up, dropped my shorts and my briefs, and leaned over the table. "Fuck me now, Eddie. Right here."

"I will never get tired of looking at that ass of yours."

"Don't just look."

He got down on his knees and began rimming me, licking and nipping at my ass, fucking me with his tongue. I moaned with pleasure as the endorphins rose in me. "Stop teasing me, Eddie. Fuck me. Now."

"Pushy bottom," he said. "Be right back."

The cold air on my wet hole made me shiver, but Eddie was back a moment later with a condom and a bottle of lube. I wanted to feel him in me, skin to skin the way we'd done in college, but I knew he'd been with too many other guys too recently to take that chance.

Thinking of Eddie with other men made my dick start to wilt, but as soon as he squirted the lube into my hole and began massaging again, I was back to iron. A moment later I felt his mushroom cap begin nosing its way into me, and I took a couple of deep breaths until the pain passed.

He stood behind me, his legs planted wide, so he could assault my hole, and his nuts banged against my skin as he drove deep into me. I started to whimper, a high-pitched message of need, and Eddie responded, piston-fucking me, accompanied by a studly monologue about how velvety smooth my ass tunnel was, how good I made him feel. "I'm your alpha male," he said, panting between thrusts. "Nobody is ever going to fuck you as well as I do."

"Less talk, more fuck," I said between moans, though in truth his sexy language got me even hotter. As he pushed into me, my dick dragged back and forth on the tabletop, an exquisite torture that I wanted to stop, but that I also wanted to go on forever.

I finally couldn't hold back any longer, and I shot my load on the table and on my groin, squeezing my ass cheeks as I came, and Eddie howled and slapped my ass and said, "Here comes papi!" He shot up inside me, and I felt the condom's reservoir swell against my prostate in a way that made me almost delirious.

He pulled out of me too soon, and when I tried to stand up, my knees were weak, and Eddie had to grab hold of me. "I'm here for you, bud," he said into my ear. "Now and forever."

Chapter 15

Two Doors Down

The morning I was to leave for Ohio with Darren, I dug through the back of my closet for all the winter clothes I'd worn in Philadelphia and New York. It was hard to remember living with so many layers. Returning to Miami had been more than a homecoming to my family; it felt like I belonged there.

What about Darren? As I packed I wondered how he felt about living in hot, humid South Florida after growing up in Ohio, college in Philly, then however long in Japan and Portland. Was this another way station for him? Or something longer?

When I picked him up at his apartment, I thought about asking him, but why? Let things evolve as they were going to. For the moment, Darren and I were together, and he looked awfully cute in a long-sleeved Penn T-shirt and tight jeans.

"You ready for this?" I asked, as we drove to the airport.

"What? For touring the factory?"

"You're going home, bud. Back to the place that made you."

"Not exactly. I don't have any plans to stop by January River. We fly in to Akron, do our thing at the factory, and retreat to the motel, where we have monkey sex all weekend until it's time to come back here."

"You aren't going to see your folks at all?"

"What's to see? My parents have both moved on. They're both remarried, with new families. Don't need me anymore."

"Darren. You can't believe that."

"And yet I do. Not everybody comes from a warm, loving family like you."

"You mean hot and smothering," I said.

"You still haven't come out to them?"

"And I don't see any reason to." I veered across a couple of lanes to get to the airport exit, and Darren gripped the door handle. "You don't think they'll suspect something when you keep getting older and never bring a girl home?" he asked. "Don't they want you to be out making babies already?"

I leaned forward, watching for the signs to the long-term parking lot. "They can think what they want. As long as I don't bring it up, they can be wilfully ignorant."

Darren shook his head.

"When did you come out to your parents?" I asked.

"I never officially did," he said. "Did they suspect something? Who knows? By the time I was a senior in high school, my mom was on like her third or fourth boyfriend since the divorce, and she hardly noticed me. When I went over to my dad's, he and his second wife were arguing all the time. I could have been cross-dressing and fucking guys in the living room, and they wouldn't have noticed."

I hated the bitterness that I heard in Darren's voice. I couldn't imagine my parents ever ignoring me that way.

After cruising down a couple of lanes, I found a spot in the parking lot, and we carried our bags over to the bus shelter. I had a backpack with my laptop and paperwork in it and a rollaboard; Darren was making do with one duffel bag he had slung over his shoulder.

"My dad went to Dartmouth, you know," he said while we waited for the shuttle bus to the airport. "So suddenly one day the fall of my senior year, he woke up and asked me where I wanted to go to college, and I shrugged and said I was figuring on Ohio State because it was cheap. He was like, no way. I was going Ivy or not at all. I looked at him. He was a sales manager for a tire company, and he was always late with his support payments to my mom, so I figured he was dead broke."

"And was he?"

"Yeah. But he's always been a street-smart guy, and he got hold of the financial aid forms and started finagling them until it was clear that I couldn't expect a penny from him or my mom. When I got into Penn, the admissions people were great, and they put together a package for me that made it work. I was able to make up whatever else I needed from working during the summer and the school year."

The bus arrived, and we stepped on. "I had no idea you were so broke," I said when we were settled at the back.

"We were all broke in college," he said. "That's why I had to stay in the dorms and on the meal plan, because financial aid covered that."

"Did you go home for summers?"

He shook his head. "Stayed in Philly. I flew back to stay with my dad for a couple of weeks after freshman year, but it was clear that I didn't fit in there anymore."

We pulled up at the terminal, went through security and found our way to the gate. While we waited, I pulled up Google Maps and found that January River wasn't far from Akron, and I began to formulate a plan to get Darren back in touch with his parents. They had to love and miss him, right?

We both worked on our laptops during the flight. As we came in for a landing, I looked out the window at the landscape. Snow dusted the tops of trees and was piled in hillocks along the roads. The Jetway was freezing, and I couldn't wait to get into the terminal and pull my coat out of my rollaboard.

"Miami boy," Darren said as I did. "This isn't cold."

"I know what cold is," I grumbled. "Four years in Philadelphia and four in New York, remember?" I looked at him. "You promised to keep me warm."

"Keep that in mind later. Now let's find the rental car desk and get moving."

We put the car in Darren's name because we figured he was the better driver in icy conditions. He didn't even need the map to get us to Barberton, taking I-77 from the airport and another highway to our motel. "You know these roads," I said.

"I grew up here, remember? If we'd gotten off at route 619 we'd have driven right through January River."

I opted for ignorance. "I didn't realize it was so close."

"So close and yet so far," Darren said. A few minutes later, he pulled the car up in front of Bill's Motel. "This is the place you booked?" It was a long single-story building that looked like it had been built in the 1940s or '50s.

"What? It was cheap," I said.

"Looks it."

We parked in front of the office and walked in together. An elderly woman with thick glasses and shoulder-length white hair was behind the desk. "I booked a room online," I said. "Gonzalez."

She peered at me. "You from Mexico?"

"Would that be a problem?"

Darren stepped up. "We're both from Miami," he said. "But I grew up in January River."

"I had kin there, long ago. All dead now." She looked down at her laptop, and I was surprised at how nimbly she typed. "Oh, there's a problem. We have you booked into a room with only one king-size bed."

"That's what I requested," I said.

"But there are two of you." She peered at us through those glasses, and I tried to remember. Was Ohio one of those red states where they tried to regulate who you could have sex with and what bathroom you could use?

"It's no problem," Darren said to her. "We're second cousins, and we grew up sharing beds together when our families went on road trips."

"Oh, well, that's all right," she said. She handed us an old-fashioned metal key on a plastic fob. "Only one key for the room, 'cause we figure it's usually one person or a married couple."

I was tempted to ask if she required a marriage license to rent to an opposite-sex couple, but I refrained.

"What was her problem?" I asked Darren as we walked back to the car. "You'd think if she was savvy enough to use a laptop and Airbnb, she wouldn't bat an eye at two guys who want to share a bed."

"We're like two doors down from Appalachia," Darren said. "About an hour and a half to the West Virginia border. Old habits die hard up here."

"You think we'll have a problem at the factory tomorrow?"

Darren shrugged. "Who knows? Let me do the talking."

We drove around town that night looking for a place to eat, and settled on a McDonald's near the I-76 highway. It wasn't healthy, but it was cheap and filling. "No after-dinner tea here," I said as we finished eating.

"I'll add this to my list of clients to approach," Darren said drily. It was still early in the evening when we got back to the motel, too early to go to sleep. At least there was Internet in the room, though it had to be accessed through a LAN cable and only one of us could be plugged in at a time.

I let Darren go online first, and sat up on the bed staring at him as he worked at the rickety desk. I loved the way his shoulders hunched as he leaned over the keyboard, the way his shirt rode down in the back and I could see a strip of his neck. I had the urge to get up and lick my way across his flesh, to feel him shiver beneath my tongue.

When he was done he pushed away from the desk. "Your turn."

"I'd rather have a turn with you." I opened my arms. "Come to papi."

"I'm tired and cranky, Eddie. Just do your online thing and let's go to sleep."

"It's only eight o'clock."

"Thank you for the time check, Siri." He turned and stalked into the bathroom.

"Jesus, what crawled up your shorts?" I muttered as the door closed behind him.

I went online, read a bunch of e-mail messages and responded to the ones I had to, and Darren was still in the bathroom. I stood up and knocked lightly on the door. "You okay?" I asked.

I heard the toilet flush and the sound of the faucet running, and then Darren opened the door. "Sorry. I needed some time to wrap my head around being back in Ohio."

I leaned forward and kissed him lightly on the lips. "You're here with me, bud. Nothing bad's going to happen to you while I'm on duty."

He smiled. "You're a sweetheart." He kissed me, pressing his lips against mine, moving forward and wrapping his arms around my waist. We kissed like that for a couple of minutes, inhaling each other's scent and feeling the dozens of points where our bodies connected.

He stuck his hands beneath my shirt and felt my skin. "You're cold," he said. "I promised to keep you warm while we're here."

"You did," I said, grinning like a fool.

We began shedding our clothes, and even though the heater was blasting, the room was still chilly and goose bumps rose on my arms. Darren noticed and began rubbing my biceps to warm them up. Pretty quickly we were naked, and I went to collapse on the ugly plaid bedspread, but Darren stopped me.

"Do you know how many germs there are on that thing? At least they probably wash the sheets between guests."

"We'll give that old bitch a reason to wash after we leave," I said. "Roll around in sweat and lube and cum."

"You're gross," Darren said, but he laughed. He pulled back the spread to reveal starched white sheets and tugged me down with him. "I want to fuck you, baby. Is that okay?"

I was usually the top, but I wasn't opposed to doing anything that made Darren happy. "You kidding? More than okay by me. But you have to do a good job to get me ready."

"I'm up for that challenge," Darren said, wagging his stiff dick at me. I reached over and grabbed a bottle of lube and a condom from my bag. I put the condom on the bed beside me and squirted some lube into Darren's hand. I faced him, spread my legs, and pulled my ass cheeks open. My dick was so hard it was standing up like a flagpole. Guess it liked the idea of me getting fucked. Or maybe it was seeing the lust flaring in Darren's brown eyes as he began fingering my hole.

The lube was cold at first, and I shivered, but very quickly it warmed up, and as the endorphins rose in my body, I didn't notice the temperature at all. I focused on the lazy circles Darren was drawing around my hole, the way his fingers tickled the wispy hairs back there.

"Can I shave your balls sometime?" Darren asked.

Kinky. "If that turns you on. Now?"

"Maybe later. Right now I have more pressing business."

He scooted up close to me so that his dick was nosing against my hole, and I took a couple of deep breaths. I didn't bottom very often so my chute was tight, and I was worried about hiding any pain.

"I'll take it easy, baby," Darren said. "You stop me whenever you need me to."

"Just do it," I said. "I can take it like a man."

More like a wimp, I thought, as he pushed his mushroom head past my anal ring, and I shuddered. It hurt like a bastard. But I could see that Darren was loving it, so I sucked it up and let him keep pushing.

It took a while, I gotta admit. Tears were starting to pool at the edges of my eyes by the time my ass finally adjusted to the intrusion. When Darren's dick banged against my prostate, I was in a whole other world. All I could think about was how much I loved him and how good he felt inside me.

Suddenly, without even realizing it, I was spewing cum all over my chest, my body racked with an orgasm made even more awesome because it was so unexpected. I writhed beneath Darren like a little slut, desperate to make him come as amazingly as I had, and as he pushed into me the headboard banged against the wall and he started moaning and crying out my name and I hoped that bitch from the front desk was on the other side of the wall, hearing every detail of how I pleased the man I loved.

Chapter 16

This is Cal

I hadn't realized how much being back in Ohio affected me until we got into that crappy motel room. In one of his drunken fits, my father had told me that he'd banged my mother in a room a lot like the one I was sharing with Eddie, before they were married, and that's when they made me.

Even years later I was still creeped out by that anecdote. My dad was lazy in many ways, and he never bothered to put on clothes if he didn't have, so I had seen his dick in person many times. As a kid I'd marveled at how much bigger his was than mine, but once I reached puberty I realized he was average.

In so many ways.

He'd always bragged about his prep school education and his Dartmouth degree. He thought he was the smartest guy in the room—and living the way he did, with bullshit jobs that didn't require more than a high school diploma, he probably was. And he moved through a string of very pretty, not so smart women, starting with my mom.

Was that why he drank so much? Bitterness over the way his life had turned out? That because he hadn't used a condom at that motel, he'd ended up trapped in a marriage he wasn't ready for, with a son he didn't want?

I was determined that I wasn't going to end up like him. I was going to follow my dreams, not get bogged down by anything. That's why I'd been so determined to accept the internship in Japan after college. Somehow I'd made a connection between my relationship with Eddie and the brief one my parents had shared, and maybe I'd used Japan as an exit strategy.

But now I was back where I'd started, in many ways. Back in Ohio, back in a relationship with Eddie Gonzalez. The world had a funny way of screwing with you. Then I remembered Eddie out there in the motel room, wanting to screw with me, and when I heard his knock on the bathroom door I was ready to get with the program.

After I'd banged the hell out of his ass, and we'd hit the wall hard enough with the headboard to leave marks, I slumped beside him and rested my head on his hairy chest. He stroked my back. "That was pretty damn awesome," he said. "I ought to bottom more often."

"I just... I don't know. I was feeling out of control, being back here."

He rubbed my shoulders with one hand. "You don't have to apologize, bud. Whatever you want to do is fine with me."

After a while we cleaned up and slid between the sheets, both of us on our side, Eddie spooning into my back, and fell asleep.

It snowed lightly overnight, and we woke to a brilliant white landscape. Even the grim line of car lots, strip shopping centers, and self-storage units looked prettier with a coating of white, though I knew from experience it would turn into a dismal gray slush very quickly.

The factory was a low-slung building in an industrial park on the outskirts of Barberton. I was surprised that the manager was a guy named Henriquez with a heavy Spanish accent. He and Eddie immediately fell into Spanglish, and I felt resentful. We were on my home turf, after all.

"What's a Cuban guy doing up here?" I whispered to Eddie while Henriquez went off to prepare a line for our viewing.

"Not Cuban, Mexican. Lots of the workers here are Mexican too."

I nodded. "So that's why the woman at the motel thought you were too."

"Yeah. Multiculturalism has hit Ohio, and Ohio doesn't seem happy about it."

"When I was growing up most people were either Irish or German, or from some part of Central Europe. A few black kids in my school, and a couple of Native Americans. Don't think I ever knew a Hispanic person before I went to Penn."

Henriquez returned and showed us the mixing and bottling stations, and it was pretty interesting. They didn't have much experience packaging dry goods like tea and herbs, but he was pretty confident that one of his lines could be adapted without much trouble.

He invited us to eat at the factory cafeteria and was proud of the way the company treated its employees. All the warning signs were in both English and Spanish, including the one that said they'd gone one hundred and eighty-three days without an accident.

It was midafternoon by the time we left the factory. "What do you want to do now?" I asked Eddie as we walked out into the parking lot, which had been plowed and salted, and the blacktop glistened.

"Find a coffee shop with Wi-Fi," Eddie said. "I like sharing with you, bud, but not so much when it comes to a single LAN cable. Do they have Starbucks in this state?"

"They have Starbucks everywhere. Even Ohio." I checked the app on my phone and found one in a shopping center off I-76, and we drove over there. Working across from Eddie, surrounded by the aroma of brewing coffee, reminded me powerfully of Miami Beach, and I realized that even though I was back in my home state, I was homesick for Florida.

We worked for a couple of hours, and then Eddie said, with a fake casualness that I detected immediately, "So, I was looking at the map, and January River isn't far."

"No, it's about a half-hour southeast of here."

"Both your parents still live there?"

"My dad does. I think my mom's on the other side of Akron. At least that's where she was the last time I had an address for her."

Eddie put his mug down on the table with a clatter. "You mean you don't know where she lives?"

I shrugged. "I haven't needed to get in touch with her. Not even sure what last name she's using." I glared at him. "Why does that matter to you?"

He shook his head. "You're weird, bud."

"I'm not weird. I don't have the relationship with my parents that you have with yours."

"I'd like to meet your father, at least. You have an address on him?"

"Why?"

"Because I want to know you. More than I already do. I realize now that we're back together how much I don't know. How you feel about stuff. Where you come from."

"I come from here. Isn't that good enough for you?"

"Fine. You don't want to see him; I'm not going to force you."

He went back to work, and I stared into space. Did I want to see my father? He and my mom had split up when I was in first grade. I lived with my mom for the next few years, until she got married again and had a new baby. She wasn't exactly the nurturing type, and my squalling little half-sister got on her nerves big-time.

I got my first hard-on when I was eleven. I had no idea what was going on down there, but I knew it felt good when I rubbed myself against my bed sheets. Because it was always dark when I did it, I didn't realize that anything was coming out of me, and it was only when I had to change the sheets that I realized there was a slight discoloration and I made the connection.

A short time after that my mom announced that I was moving in with my dad and his girlfriend, who had two boys of her own, three and five years older than I was. I thought at the time that she'd figured out what I was doing, that it was wrong, and I was being punished for it.

Later I realized she was overwhelmed and needed to lighten her load, and my dad had stepped up to the plate.

My dad was living in his girlfriend's house in January River then. It was a run-down bungalow, with two bedrooms and one bathroom. Ricky and Robby had bunk beds in one room, my dad and his girlfriend in the other. My dad got hold of a cot and put it in the boys' room for me, and I lived jammed in with them for the next year and a half.

They were both totally straight but very randy boys, and they talked about sex all the time. They'd ask me questions about sex and tell me I was all wrong, and proceed to give me all kinds of wacky information in the hopes that I'd embarrass myself someday. I remember seeing ads for a jockstrap brand named Bike, and asking them what that term meant.

Ricky went into a long elaborate story of a man on top of a woman pedaling his legs while he fucked her, and even though I was pretty naive I knew he was shitting me. I didn't understand why athletic supporters turned me on so much—at least not until later.

They had worn copies of old *Playboy* and *Hustler* magazines, and sometimes they'd pull them out and show me the pictures and ask me to tell them what was going on. I was mortified when my dick reacted more to the naked men than the women, but neither of them seemed to notice.

My dad and his girlfriend were both drinking a lot, and so were Ricky and Robby. They kept trying to get me to drink with them, but I hated the smell and I was worried what I'd do if I lost control of my urges.

The fights between my dad and his girlfriend escalated until finally one day he told me to pack my bags. We stayed at a motel for a week; then he rented us a house on the other side of town. *"We'll be bachelors together,"* he'd said, but it was only a few months before he started dating another woman, this one much younger, and she moved in with us. At least this woman didn't have any kids of her own.

I saw my mom only infrequently through those years, always afraid that if she saw how well-behaved I was, she'd want me living with her again. Whenever my parents were together, I heard the term "child support" thrown around, along with his insistence that he wasn't going to pay her a penny.

The last time we'd spoken was a few days before I left for Japan, and he'd told me he was proud of me. That now that I had an Ivy League degree, the world was my oyster.

I'd wanted to say, yeah, dad, like your degree did for you, but I didn't say anything.

Almost against my will, I looked up property records in January River, and sure enough, he was still the owner of that house. I found a marriage license online from a few years before, and a divorce decree a year after the marriage. A landline was registered at the house, so I figured that meant he still lived there.

I didn't tell Eddie what I'd found, though. I knew that if I did, he'd force me to call my dad, even go over there, and I didn't want that.

Or did I? Around five o'clock, we were wrapping up and Eddie asked what I wanted to do for dinner. I remembered a place I'd gone a couple of times with my dad, on the outskirts of January River, an old country-style place that served burgers and ribs, and my mouth watered.

I realized I wasn't kidding anybody. "Let me make a call." I picked up my cell and punched in my dad's home number. I didn't expect him to answer, but I'd leave a message.

Instead I heard his voice. "This is Cal."

"Dad?" My voice cracked. "It's Darren. I'm in Barberton on business, and I thought I might stop by and see you."

Chapter 17

Worthy's

Darren surprised the hell out of me when he called his father. I only heard his side of the conversation, but it sounded like his dad was glad to hear from him, and eager to meet him for dinner at a place called Worthy's.

When he ended the call, Darren looked at me. "Satisfied now?"

"Only if you are." But I was glad that he'd gotten a good response. I could see that he was hurting, and I wanted to make it better for him —but it wasn't up to me.

It took us about a half hour to reach the restaurant, which either had been decorated like an old shack, or actually was one. It had a tumbledown look, the outside peppered with old license plates, and the smell of barbecue wafted through the air.

Darren parked, and we walked up to the front door of the restaurant. The door opened, and an older version of Darren stepped out. He had the same green eyes and floppy brown hair, although the man's was tinged with gray, and there were crow's feet around his eyes. But he was a handsome guy and I could see from looking at him the way that Darren would age.

"This my father, Calvin Carter," Darren said.

"Call me Cal." His father's handshake was strong.

"Eddie Gonzalez," I said. "Pleased to meet you."

"Eddie and I went to Penn together, and now we're working together on a business," Darren said, as we walked inside the restaurant. "We came to Ohio to look at a production facility."

"That's my boy," Cal said. "Always sharp as a tack." The restaurant was decorated like an old country cabin, with rough wooden walls and all kinds of kitschy crap, from rusted metal signs to fishing rods and what looked like a moonshine still in one corner.

Cal bypassed the hostess stand and the sign that said PLEASE WAIT TO BE SEATED. He led us forward. "Come on; I've got my favorite table."

A busty waitress with peroxide-blonde hair hailed us as we walked past. "Hey, Cal, honey," she said. She was about Cal's age, late forties or early fifties, and she wore a yellow and white uniform with a big bow that tied at the back.

"How's it going, Etta," he said. "This is my boy Darren and his friend."

"Aren't you the spitting image of your pop," Etta said. "You boys sit down, and I'll bring you some menus. I know Cal don't need one 'cause he never orders anything but the fried catfish and hush puppies."

"You still come here a lot, Dad?" Darren asked as we sat down.

"Couple of times a week. Can't beat them for food and prices."

Etta arrived with the menus a moment later, along with a big glass of sweet tea for Cal and tumblers of ice water for both Darren and me. "I'll have a sweet tea too," Darren said, though I said I'd stick with the water. I couldn't imagine what tea would taste like in a place like that, or why in the world Darren, who was a tea snob if there ever was one, would order it.

I looked at the menu, a single laminated sheet with the same graphics as on the walls. They had "kuntry" fried steak, fried okra, and baked "po-taters." It was like I'd dropped into an alternate reality.

At Cal's suggestion, we all got the catfish, though I asked for macaroni and cheese with mine instead of the black-eyed peas and rice and gravy that Darren and his father ordered. I was a Cuban boy, after all, and no way was I eating some bastardized version of beans and rice in a goofy place in Ohio.

"So tell me about this business you're starting," Cal said after Etta left. "Something Japanese? Import-export?" He looked at me. "My boy was always fascinated with that stuff, ever since he was a kid. Couldn't figure it out for the life of me."

I could see Darren trying to figure out how to describe the business, so I jumped in. "Back in college, Darren turned me on to drinking tea," I said. "I had a part-time job bartending, and I started playing around with mixing tea and liquor into cocktails."

I told him about moving to Wall Street, starting my business, and hooking up with Phil Sweet, who re-introduced me to Darren.

By then Darren knew what he wanted to say. "I always liked drinking sweet tea with you, Dad. But you can't get it in Japan or in Portland, so I started mixing my own, and one day I gave some to a friend who worked in a restaurant. He asked if I could mix some up for his customers, and when we sat down to look at his menu I realized there were other tea mixes I could put together depending on what the customer had for dinner or dessert."

"And all that from drinking sweet tea with your old dad," Cal said and smiled. "Always knew you were a go-getter, boy. That's why I knew you weren't going to Ohio State. Only the Ivy League for my boy." He looked at me. "You come from college stock, Eddie?"

"Nope. First one in family to get a college degree in the States, though back in Cuba, my great-uncle had a law degree. He was a political activist, though, so Castro had him put in prison and killed. That's what triggered my family to move here."

We chatted off and on during the meal. "So, you're living in Miami now," Cal said. "Must be nice, all those pretty ladies in skimpy bathing suits."

"Dad, I'm gay," Darren said. "Come on; you've always known that. So is Eddie. He's my boyfriend as well as my business partner."

Talk about spilling the beans over rice and beans.

Cal shrugged. "Yeah, but you never said anything. So I thought you were just, you know. Kind of effeminate, kind of shy. Figured it would take the right woman to squeeze it out of you."

Cal looked at me. "You treating my boy well?"

"Absolutely," I said. "Darren's the kindest person I know, and one of the smartest. It's been great working with him."

Darren looked at me like I had surprised him.

"You boys are careful, aren't you?" Cal asked. "You don't need to get AIDS or Hepatitis C or any of that other crap that's going around."

Cal hadn't said anything about his own romantic life, but I figured that if he was aware of all the STDs out there, he was probably taking his own precautions. "Yes, sir," I said, though Darren was rolling his eyes.

"Well, that's good," Cal said. "Now, how about pie? They make a pretty damn good peach cobbler here."

We ordered three different kinds of pie—peach, blueberry, and pecan, and shared them among us. I didn't know what I'd been expecting from Cal Carter, but he'd turned out to be a lot better than what I expected from what Darren had said.

"You ever speak to your mother?" Cal asked, as he sat back after demolishing the pie on his plate.

"Not for years," Darren said. "You?"

Cal shook his head. "Once you were out of high school, there was no reason for us to talk anymore. I want to say that woman was mistake number one in my life of romance, but then I wouldn't have gotten you."

"You have other kids, don't you, Dad? How's Destiny?"

"Don't see her much. You know I never married her mother, and she wouldn't put my name on the birth certificate, so I don't have any legal rights. Her mother married a man and took Dessie to California a few years ago. No other kids except her, at least that I know of."

Cal had a hangdog look on his face, and I felt sorry for him, though I had a feeling that at least in the past he hadn't been very careful about where he spread his seed. Etta came back with the check, which Cal insisted on paying, and the two of them bantered for a moment or two. "She's a sweet gal," Cal said when she was gone. "Keep trying to get her to go out with me, but she says no. I'm not giving up, though."

When we walked back to the parking lot, Cal shook my hand and turned to Darren. "Don't be such a stranger, son," he said, and hugged Darren.

We got back into the rental car. "That wasn't so awful, was it?" I asked.

"Of course it was," Darren said. "Are you an idiot?"

"What do you mean? Your father was very cool about you being gay."

He turned to look at me. "It's not all about you or me." He backed out of the parking space and turned savagely toward the road and didn't say anything more for the rest of the ride.

When we got back to the room, I turned the heater on high and asked Darren, "You want to tell me what you're so pissed off about?"

"Did you look at him?"

"Of course I did. He looks like an older version of you. Handsome guy, charming."

"You didn't see the frayed cuff on his shirt? The yellow stain under his arm? Those red veins on his nose?"

"So he's not a snazzy dresser, maybe he drinks a little. What's wrong with that?"

"You don't know my father. He never went out of the house unless he looked perfect. Used to iron his shirts himself because no woman could ever do it to his satisfaction. And the car he was driving? The old Toyota with the banged-up fender? He always drove fancy cars. 'You can tell a lot about a man from the car he drives,' he used to say."

"So you're saying he's broke? We shouldn't have let him pay the bill?"

"I'm saying he's gone downhill. Probably drinking too much. And what was he doing at home on a weekday afternoon? Did he lose his job?"

I flopped onto the bed, despite Darren's dire warnings about the flowered comforter. "Why don't you ask him these questions?"

"It would kill him if he knew that I knew he was in trouble."

Darren went into the bathroom and closed the door hard behind him. Had I made the wrong decision in pushing him to see his father? I'd thought the dinner went so well, been impressed at how easily Cal had accepted Darren's sexuality. But obviously I'd been wrong.

I got up and plugged the LAN cable into my laptop and began going through e-mails. In one of them, Phil Sweet had recommended a guy in San Francisco who was a freelance rep for liquor manufacturers. *You're going to need people to sell your product to grocery chains and liquor stores,* he wrote. *This guy might be a good start.*

I clicked through to the man's LinkedIn profile, and I was suitably impressed. I started Googling to get a sense of how we'd pay someone like that, and what they'd earn. I realized that we'd already incorporated a figure like that into our projections without ever thinking about how we'd fill those positions.

Darren came out of the bathroom and sat beside me. "I'm sorry I yelled at you."

"You didn't yell. I wasn't seeing the big picture, and you pointed it out to me."

He nodded, then leaned over and kissed my cheek. "You're a sweetheart."

"So are you."

He looked at what I'd been reading. "Sales reps? For us?"

I explained what Phil had written. "I was thinking maybe you could ask your dad if he'd be interested," I said.

Darren shook his head. "He's an alcoholic. Sending him to bars would be crazy."

"How do you know that he's an alcoholic? He didn't have any liquor at dinner. Did you smell anything on his breath?"

"No. But just because he didn't drink today doesn't mean he's not an alcoholic."

"Have you ever asked him?"

Darren pursed his lips but didn't say anything.

"And you said yourself you've hardly seen him for the last ten years or so. Don't be so quick to pass judgment, bud. And he wouldn't go to the individual bars, would he? To wholesalers and corporate headquarters. He's got a lot of charm."

I logged off my accounts and unplugged the LAN cable. "Your turn. I'm going to chill."

I went back to the bed, and Darren turned to his laptop. He worked for a half hour or so, then shut down. He pulled down the covers and sat on the sheets. "I think it would be too weird," he said. "My dad working for me."

"If that's the problem, I could manage the sales staff, and you could handle production. I'm already planning to handle all the numbers."

He leaned back against the pillows. "We'll see."

The heater had kicked in, and I was feeling warm in my shirt and sweater, so I stood up and started to take my clothes off.

Darren turned to look at me. "I don't think I'll ever get tired of seeing you strip."

"Really?" I was naked from the waist up, but still wearing my slacks, boxers, and socks. I began to sway my hips, and Darren smiled.

I reached for my phone and pulled up a playlist of Cuban music. At the distinctive sound of the claves—two sticks beaten together to establish a rhythm—I got into the music, moving my hips in the way I had learned at countless family parties.

"You are so damn sexy," Darren said, his voice hoarse.

"I bet I can make you come without even touching you," I said.

"I'll take that bet."

I shimmied my slacks off, then picked off my socks, so I was dancing in my bare feet and my boxers. My dick was stiff and pressing against the fabric, and I could tell Darren was heating up when he opened his pants and let his dick free.

It was a turn-on to me to see him start fisting his dick, the precum oozing from the slit, his eyes glazing over with lust. I pulled down my boxers, and my dick popped up, banging against my stomach as I danced. I began tweaking my own nipple with one hand, jerking myself with the other.

Darren was definitely getting into the show, panting heavily as he rubbed one out. I moved over close to the bed, so my dick was at his mouth. "Suck me, baby," I said.

"I thought you weren't going to touch me," Darren said, but he opened his jaws.

"I won't touch your dick. But I want your hot mouth."

I gave up dancing as he enveloped me. He kept jerking himself as he sucked me, and all at once his jaws went slack, and he yipped in pleasure as he came. Then he went right back to me, and a moment or two later I was spewing down his throat.

"We make a beautiful partnership," I said, as I sagged back.

Darren wiped his lips. "We work this way. The jury is still out on the tea business."

"Who are those jurors?" I said. "Let me suck them, one by one." I picked up his right hand, still sticky with his cum, and slid it into my mouth.

Chapter 18

Parker's Problem

I drove us back to the Akron airport in the rental car on Sunday morning. There was only a single terminal, nothing as elaborate as most of the airports I'd passed through in my life, but I could still remember my father dropping me off there for my flight to Philadelphia the first time I left for Penn.

He'd been so proud that day, but I'd been too nervous to see it. *"You be good out there, Darren,"* he had said. *"Make me proud."*

But I'd been too worried about how I'd survive on my own to say anything other than, *"Thanks, Dad."*

Now I might be in a position to help him, by hiring him as our manufacturer's rep. I knew he could charm anyone if he set his mind to it, and that he had the skills to handle the job.

While we waited for our flight to Charlotte, with continuing service to Miami, I paced around the waiting area, thinking about my relationship with my father. Why had I shut him out for so long?

Seeing him through Eddie's eyes, I realized he wasn't a bad guy. Was I disappointed in him—with his charm and his brains, why hadn't he been more successful? Made more money, given me a better childhood?

That was a selfish attitude and while it was part of the story, it wasn't the whole thing. I had been confused as a teenager, aware of my same-sex attraction and at the same time knowing how society looked down on it. I'd internalized that homophobia, and only been able to let go of it when I got to college.

Had I assumed my father would feel that way, and shut him out rather than giving him a chance? But we'd never communicated much. He saved all his charm for the ladies he romanced and the clients he schmoozed. By the time he got home, there was little pleasantry left for me, especially if I was sullen and moody.

I'd gradually developed that habit of shutting down emotionally, failing to communicate. It had caused the demise of my first relationship with Eddie, when I didn't know how to talk to him about my desire to go to Japan. Had I learned anything since then? Could I at least start by opening a channel of communication with my father, forcing myself to say the things I had to, believing that because he loved me, and I loved him, each of us in our own way, that we'd muddle through?

"Darren. Sit down," Eddie said, as I passed him for the third or fourth time. "Why are you so antsy?"

I settled into the molded plastic seat beside him. "It's been a strange weekend," I said. "Thanks for what you did, pushing me to see my father. I still need to process everything that's happened, but I'll consider asking him to be a rep for us."

"You don't have to do anything you don't want to," Eddie said.

"And I appreciate your saying that, but right now I'm still struggling to figure out what it is I want." I looked over at him. "Other than you, of course."

He smiled, and I loved the way his eyes widened a bit, as if happiness was trying to push out of them too. The gate agent called our flight. As we flew, we both went back over the brochures we'd been given at the manufacturing plant.

"I'm concerned about the payment terms," Eddie said, pointing at the relevant section. "What if we have some cash flow problems, and they hold our merchandise hostage?"

"It's up to us to make sure we don't have that kind of problem, isn't it?" I responded. I was more concerned about the restriction they had on receiving raw materials. "What if it snows and the delivery truck is late bringing in goods? If they shut down every day at five o'clock, whole loads of merchandise could be ruined."

We agonized over those problems through the wait in Charlotte and the flight to Miami, making endless notes about questions for Phil and whoever he could refer us to who had experience with the factory in Barberton.

It was a relief to get off the plane in Miami and be able to focus on something simple, like getting out of the terminal and back to the long-term lot where Eddie had parked. We turned our phones back on in the shuttle to the lot, and mine buzzed frantically with missed calls and messages.

"Who's that?" Eddie asked.

"Parker. He's not usually this hyper. Let me see what's up."

I listened to the messages as the bus meandered through the airport property, and by the time we'd reached Eddie's car, I was pretty horrified. "One of Parker's clients was arrested on Friday for shooting up a school," I said, as I stowed the phone back in my pocket.

"That's grim. Here in Miami?" he asked, as we stepped off the bus.

"Uh-huh. We must have missed all the news while we were away. The police came to Parker's apartment this morning. This guy says that he told Parker what he was going to do, and Parker didn't stop him. So now the police want to arrest Parker as an accessory."

"Holy shit. Can they do that?"

"Don't know. I need to call Parker." I looked over at Eddie. "Will you mind?"

"Not at all. He's still your friend, right? And he needs you."

"I appreciate that." We loaded our bags into Eddie's trunk and took off as I called Parker. He sounded pretty frantic, and I spent most of the drive to my apartment trying to calm him down. By the time we got there, it was clear I needed to go over to Parker's place.

"Call me later. Let me know what's going on and if I can do anything to help," Eddie said, as we pulled up in front of my building.

"I will." I leaned over and kissed him. "This weekend was good."

"Only good?" Eddie said with mock horror.

"It was Ohio," I said. "Good is a superlative when the Buckeye State is concerned."

He laughed, and I dragged my bag upstairs, not even bothering to unpack. I jumped into my car and headed over to the mainland, to the apartment Parker rented in a complex off US 1 in North Miami.

"I'm sorry to bother you, but I didn't know who else to call," he said, as I walked in. "I'm not allowed to talk about this with anyone I work with and none of my other friends are smart enough to help me figure things out."

I wasn't sure what that said about either me or Parker, but I let it slide. "What happened?"

He wiped away tears and blew his nose. "I shouldn't tell you my client's name, but you can find it in all the news reports. And I probably shouldn't tell you any of the details of our conversations, but I don't know how else to process this."

"Could you speak to somebody where you went to school? A professor you studied with?"

"I'm afraid to, because what if it turns out I did something wrong? They could be required to report me, or testify against me."

I took a deep breath. "Tell me the whole story."

We sat down, him on the sofa, me on the chair across from him. "My agency has a deal with a couple of different colleges," he said. "We get referrals from students who are having problems, and the college insurance pays for the first couple of visits. Most of the students I help are having problems with money, or relationships, or general depression. We talk about coping strategies, and I refer them to agencies that can help with family services, transportation issues, and financial aid screw-ups."

"Sounds good."

"It is. We help a lot of people. When I first met Jarvis, I could see he had a whole range of issues, but you have to start small. He had problems with anger management and depression, and he was acting out in class. I referred him to a mental health clinic where he could get a diagnosis and medication."

"So isn't anything he did their issue?"

He shook his head. "Psychiatrists these days don't talk to you about your problems. It's not like Freud and lying down on a couch. You're depressed? Here's a prescription. You're anxious? Here's a different one. You have learning difficulties, trouble sleeping? There's a pill for everything these days."

"So Jarvis went to the psychiatrist and got pills," I said, and Parker nodded. "Then what?"

"He kept coming in to talk to me. He'd get very agitated, even on the meds. The professors were out to get him. The other students were rude. The school was a rip-off, and he'd never be able to get a job. Lots of anger."

"And?"

"And I tried to counsel him. He was in a criminal justice program, and we looked at different career paths. He had a job as a security guard at a condo complex, but he had a lot of problems with co-workers, and he got fired. I managed to pull some strings and get him hired at an office building that needed someone on night duty, where he'd be on his own and not have to work with anyone else."

I was feeling tired and dehydrated after the flight from Ohio, but I didn't want to interrupt Parker to get myself a glass of water or make us both some tea.

Parker's shoulders shook, and he started to sob. "I should have done more for him," he said.

I moved over to sit beside him and put my arms around his shoulders. "You did what you could."

"But it wasn't enough. Friday morning he went to the campus of this college to talk to the dean about dropping out. They told him that it was already too late in the term. And that if he dropped out, he'd have to pay back his financial aid before he could take any more courses."

Parker took a deep breath. "Apparently he went home and got a gun, then returned to the campus. He parked and started walking to the dean's office, shooting at people as he went."

"Oh my God," I said. I'd heard about similar events at other places but having left college only a few years before, the idea that someone could start randomly shooting on a campus still freaked me out.

"Fortunately he's a lousy shot," Parker said. "He wounded a half dozen people before campus security showed up. One of the guards shot him, and they managed to get him down and disarmed. After he was booked, he started blaming everything on me, that he'd told me what he was going to do, and I'd said he should go ahead."

"Of course you wouldn't say that," I said.

"I know that, and you know that, but the police don't. They came here first thing this morning, banging on the door and demanding to talk to me. The detective kept asking me questions, and I started to get confused. He finally left but said that I could be charged as an accessory if I'd known about Jarvis's plans and didn't stop him or report him."

"Did you know he was angry at the college?"

"Yes. And I told him to speak to them about withdrawing. But he never said anything about going there and shooting people."

"Then you can't be blamed for not reporting him," I said, though I wasn't sure that was the case.

We talked for another hour, Parker going over everything he'd done with Jarvis, every action, every statement, and everything he didn't do. We were cuddled up close and my shoulder was damp with his tears.

"You're such a kind person, Darren," he said. "I was trying to be all adult and calm when we broke up, but I miss you so much. Isn't there anything I can do to get you back again?"

"Parker..."

Before I could say too much he was kissing me, leaning forward and reaching down to rub my stiffening dick. I tried to pull away, but he wouldn't let me go. "Please, Darren? Be with me tonight, even if you can't stay forever."

I couldn't tell him that I'd picked up again with Eddie, days after breaking up with him. But I couldn't cheat on Eddie either. What was I supposed to do?

Chapter 19

Tío Eduardo

As I drove back to South Beach after dropping Darren off at his place, I was encouraged by how well Cal Carter had taken the revelation that his son was gay. Was that just him? Or were the winds of change sweeping through Miami too? Could I come out to my parents, introduce them to Darren?

I looked at the clock on my dashboard. Like many Latin families, mine tended to eat late, and if I went directly to Westchester, I'd get home in time for dinner. My mouth watered at the memory of my mom's beans and rice, so different from the bland watery stuff I'd tasted from Darren's plate at Worthy's.

I didn't even have to call and say I was coming over. There was always enough food, always a place at the table for me. Or at least there was now. Would I still be welcome if I told them the truth? I knew other guys from Caribbean backgrounds who'd had terrible problems.

A high school friend had come over from the Dominican Republic to stay with his older sister, and when he'd come out, she'd kicked him to the curb with only a plastic garbage bag of his clothes and toiletries. Jean-Pierre, the Haitian guy from the brew pub, had been a junior at FIU when his parents discovered gay porn on his laptop computer. They hadn't kicked him out, but they'd raged at him for months because they were so angry that he'd turned out that way.

A Colombian guy who tended bar at one of the restaurants I sold to had confided that he'd been arrested back in Bogotá after the police discovered him having sex with another man in a public park. His parents had refused to bail him out, and he'd been raped in jail. As soon as he got out, he'd fled for the United States.

But I also knew guys who'd had an easier time of it. My college friend Raul's parents were both born in Spain, then immigrated to Cuba, where he was born. They'd come to the US when he was a kid, and they'd known that he was gay and been fine with it.

As I navigated the local streets toward my parents' house, I tried to remember other positive stories, but I couldn't come up with others. All the gay Latinos I knew in Miami were estranged from their families, either by their decision or their families'. Would I end up like one of them?

Suddenly I knew that it didn't matter. I had to be who I was, to live honestly in the world. And as long as I had Darren by my side, I'd be able to succeed.

Getting back together with him had energized me. We were good together—better than good, great. Sure, we pushed each other's buttons sometimes, but that was the beauty of love—you helped the other person become the best version of himself.

"*Ay, my hijo!*" my mother exclaimed when I walked inside. "*¡Qué linda sorpresa!* I thought you were in Ohio."

I still had a key to the front door, and I never would have considered ringing the bell like a stranger. I had a momentary image of my father demanding I return the key, but I pushed it away.

"I was," I said. I leaned down to kiss her cheek. "But I missed your Moros y Cristianos so as soon as I landed, I had to come over."

"*¡Ay, dios mio!* I don't have any. I could make some for you, but it will take a while."

"That's okay. Anything you cook is awesome."

"Next time, you tell me you are coming," she said, waggling her finger at me. "Ramon! Look who is here! *Tu hijo!*"

My father came out of the kitchen eating a *pastelito,* a round meat pastry my mom served as an appetizer. He hugged me, and I had to explain again why I'd come straight from the airport. We sat down to dinner in our regular places, my parents at opposite ends of the table—my mother closest to the kitchen—Connie and me on one side, my abuela on the other.

Abuela looked great, considering she'd just celebrated her eightieth birthday. Her hair was puffed up and lacquered like a hot air balloon, and even though it was a Sunday evening at home, she was wearing dark red lipstick and big false eyelashes.

I came from a line of good-looking people, I thought, as I surveyed my family. My mom and Connie both had dark hair, big, expressive eyes, and cupid's-bow lips. My dad was still ruggedly handsome, without the gray that I'd noticed on Cal Carter.

"What did you do in Ohio?" Connie asked as we ate.

I explained about the factory visit. "And my friend Darren, my business partner, he was with me," I said. "He comes from Ohio, and we stopped by to visit his father while we were there."

"This is the Darren you were so close to in college?" my mother asked. "The one with the tea?"

I was surprised that she'd remembered but before I could answer she added, "*Por supuesto*—he is the reason you started this tea business, isn't he?"

"Well, not the reason," I said. "I mean, I started drinking tea with him back at Penn, but Cockteals was my idea."

"Stupid name," my father muttered. "Makes it sound like you are preparing drinks for roosters, or maricónes."

Something snapped inside me. "And is that a bad thing?" I asked. "Making drinks for maricónes? Men like me?"

The room got deadly quiet. Then my abuela said, "Your tío Eduardo, he loved his mojitos." She smiled at us. "So picky too. The mint had to be fresh picked. And only Havana Club rum, the real rum from the island, before *ese cerdo,* Fidel, took over the factory."

We all looked at abuela like she was crazy. Or was she trying to distract us from my revelation?

"*¿Que?*" she asked. "My brother was a maricón. So? I loved him. So did you, Ramon. You wanted to be like him, with his white suits and his straw hats and his French cologne."

"Tío Eduardo was not a maricón," my father insisted.

Abuela laughed. "Why do you think Castro arrested him and put him in the camp?"

"He was a political activist," my father said. "That's what you always said."

"*Claro que si.* But the group he ran, it was a group of homosexuals who wanted their rights. That is why Castro had to make him stop. Those cigars Fidel always smoked? You think that was just for the aroma?"

Despite the turmoil raging inside me, I couldn't help laughing that my grandmother was suggesting Fidel had an oral fixation because he favored cigars. "If that's the case, Abuela, then a lot of Cuban men feel the same way."

She laughed merrily.

My father abruptly pushed back his chair and left the kitchen. Connie looked at me. "You make dinner interesting, Eddie. You should come by more often."

A moment later, my father returned, holding the framed photograph of Tío Eduardo that sat on a shelf in the living room. He stared at it and looked at me. Then back at the photo.

I knew it well. Tío Eduardo stood by a 1950s model car on a street in Havana. He cut a very dashing figure in his well-cut white suit, white shirt, and blood-red bow tie. His white Panama hat was tilted at a rakish angle, and he had one well-polished patent-leather oxford on the car's running board. A cigar dangled loosely from one corner of his mouth.

No one said anything.

"Sit down and finish eating, mi hijo," Abuela said. "*La comida se está enfriando.*" She picked up her fork and began eating again, and so did my mother, my sister, and I. After a long moment, my father sat down, put the photo down in the center of the table, and picked up his fork.

Before he went back to eating, though, he said, "This Darren. He is not Spanish, is he?"

"German and Scotch-Irish, I think," I said. My mouth was dry, and I picked up my tumbler of water.

"You'll bring him to dinner next week," my mother said. She shook her head. "*Un otro Americano.* Connie, you bring your friend too. We will have to teach them both Spanish."

Connie turned slightly sideways and looked at me. She smiled, and I smiled back. Spanish lessons. I'd have to practice with Darren before next Sunday. I could see my father wasn't fully reconciled to my sexuality, but at least he hadn't kicked me out of the house.

The dinner wasn't over yet, though. And from the way my father brooded at the head of the table, I knew I wasn't out of the woods by a long shot.

Chapter 20

Welcome Mat

I spent the night at Parker's apartment, in his bed, with him snuggled up close to me. No sex, but we were still more intimate than I wanted to tell Eddie about. He had called the night before, but I hadn't answered, and his voice mail message hadn't been very specific—only a demand that I call him as soon as possible.

Parker had a meeting with his supervisor first thing in the morning, so after I forced him to eat a blueberry muffin and have a cup of tea, he went off to work and I went home. I was tired of traveling and wanted to be in my own space.

There was a single washer-dryer in the basement of my building, and fortunately it wasn't in use when I dragged my big plastic basket of dirty laundry down there. I put the clothes in the washer and leaned back against the counter. The room was hot and muggy and as I watched my shirts and underwear tumble around, I tried to make sense of everything that had happened in the past few days.

I'd signed a deal with Phil Sweet to provide funding to take my tea business to the next level. I'd welcomed Eddie Gonzalez back into my life and into my bed. I'd come out to my dad, and I'd comforted Parker through the start of what was sure to be a tough time.

How did I feel about all that? I was excited, sure. Scared. Horny as all get out. And strangely relieved too. My life was beginning to take shape, after five years drifting through Japan and Portland, trying to figure out what my grownup goals were.

And of course, there had been a sad undercurrent in my life, one that I was only now beginning to recognize. Missing Eddie. Missing a relationship with my father. Both of those had begun to improve.

I left my laundry to do its business and went back up to my apartment, where I called Eddie. "You must have been exhausted by the time you got home," he said. "I called you and texted you, but I didn't hear anything back."

"Yeah, Parker was a real mess, and he wore me out," I said. "So what's up?"

"I came out to my family last night."

I nearly dropped the phone. "What brought that on?"

"It was obviously something that had been bubbling inside me, but this weekend, being back together with you, seeing you and your dad, it all boiled up and I went right over there after I dropped you off."

"How did your parents take it?"

"My dad wasn't real happy, and my mom didn't say much. But my abuela was cool. Get this. My great-uncle, you know, the one I'm named after? He was gay too."

"How did that come up?"

He explained about his grandmother, and some photo of his uncle, and his father, and honestly I wasn't concentrating that closely. I was trying to figure out what I should tell him about Parker. But the topic never came up again, so I left it at what I'd said.

"You want to get together today?" Eddie asked. "I want to go over those income and expense projections again before we meet with Phil on Wednesday."

"Honestly? I'm beat, and I'm worried this thing with Parker is going to keep going for a while." I told him about Parker's meeting with his boss. "And I have some new orders I have to fill, and one of my clients is revamping their menu and wants a consultation."

"That's cool," Eddie said. "I've got my own stuff to handle too. Hope things work out for Parker House Rolls."

I laughed. "Yeah, I'll let him know you're concerned."

"Does he know that we're back together?"

"No. And now isn't a good time to tell him."

We agreed to check in with each other that evening. I answered some e-mails, moved my laundry from the washer to the dryer. As I was walking back upstairs, I ran into Parker. He looked like a boy on the verge of a nervous breakdown. His eyes were red and his hands were shaking. He launched himself into my arms on the stairway.

He choked on his sobs as he tried to explain what had happened that morning, but I quieted him and led him upstairs. "I'm sus—suspended," he said, catching his breath a couple of times. "With pay, but only for a week."

"Calm down. I'll make some tea." I pulled out a box of my chamomile mix and began to boil a pot of water. "What happens next?"

"The police are getting a warrant to view the records of my meetings with Jarvis," he said, his hands twisting over each other. "My boss is going to look over them first and make sure that I followed all the right standards and procedures."

"And did you?"

"I don't know," he said, anguish in his voice. "What if I did something wrong? What if I missed something? I could lose my job. I could go to prison!"

I pulled a chair beside his and sat down. "You're not going to prison, Parker." I put my arm around his shoulder, and he leaned against me.

"You don't know that." He snuffled into my shoulder.

"I know you, and that you're a good person. You wouldn't do anything to harm a client, and if you knew there was a credible threat, I'm sure you would react appropriately."

The teakettle began to whistle, and I stood up. "Tell that to the police," Parker said.

I picked up the kettle to stop the noise, but before I poured the water into the teapot I turned to him. "Are they going to talk to me?"

"I don't know. They asked for the names of everyone I might have spoken to about Jarvis."

"But you didn't say anything to me until after he was already arrested," I said.

As I turned back to the teapot and poured the boiling water over the infuser filled with the chamomile mix, I tried to remember if Parker had ever told me anything about his clients. I didn't think so. He had always been very professional. Even when he was visibly upset after a client meeting, he wouldn't tell me anything about what was bothering him.

Of course, I hadn't pressed him either. Was that because I respected his professional responsibilities? Or because I didn't care? Parker was a sweet guy, and we'd had fun together, but I'd never felt the emotional bond with him that I had with Eddie.

I poured tea for both of us, and by the time he'd finished two cups, Parker was much calmer. I sent him into my bedroom to take a nap, and I set up my kitchen table so that I could fulfill the orders that had come in while Eddie and I were in Ohio. I loved the way the teas and herbs smelled as I weighed them and packaged them in individual sachets, then stacked the bags in simple white paper boxes.

Back in Portland, I'd hired a friend with some serious graphic arts skills to design a logo for me—a cascade of colorful herbs and tea leaves falling into an infuser set above a teapot of boiling water. Tendrils of steam rose from the water and curled around the words "Tea by D," the name of my business.

Pretty lame, I thought, as I peeled labels and placed them on boxes. I regularly printed up sheets of labels identifying exactly what was in each mix, with my logo and website. The only people who ever saw those labels were the servers, and sometimes sous chefs, who brewed the tea, but I'd never considered them much of a sales tool.

That was going to have to change. Eddie and I needed a new company name and logo, one that would pop off grocery and liquor store shelves. How were we going to get across both of our angles?

I hated Eddie's business name, Cockteals, because it was stupid and sounded too gay, but I had to admit at least it had some flair. Tea by D was boring.

Like me without Eddie.

He brought something out in me I couldn't quantify. I felt more alive around him, and I was sure that came through in my presentations to Phil Sweet. I was passionate about tea, of course, and that came through when I spoke to clients and pitched my products. But the rest of the time I was as bland as a bag of Lipton's.

It was going to be a challenge, for sure. My brain kept circling around packaging and logo ideas as I finished the orders, and occasionally I'd stop to scribble out an idea or make an attempt at a logo. My art skills were sadly lacking, and everything I did looked like the work of a second-grader who could barely grip a crayon.

I got so caught up in what I was doing that I forgot that Parker was even in the apartment. Then someone knocked on my front door.

Was it the police? Would I need a lawyer myself? How could I pay legal fees when I was barely scraping out a living?

I went to the door, and I was relieved to see through the peephole that it was only Eddie. "Thank God it's you," I said, as I leaned forward to kiss him.

"Who were you expecting? The Grim Reaper?"

"Is it the police?"

We both turned at the sound of Parker's voice. He'd come out of my bedroom in his bland white boxer briefs, and he was rubbing the sleep from his eyes.

Eddie looked from him to me. "I didn't realize I'd be interrupting anything." He shook his head. "Jeez. I never figured you for this kind of guy, Darren. Spend the weekend with me and immediately jump back into bed with Mr. Rolls. Guess there's a lot we still don't know about each other. And that doesn't make for a very good partnership, does it?"

He turned on his heel and stalked back toward the stairs. I followed him into the hallway. "Eddie. It's not what you think. Parker's wiped out. He was taking a nap."

"Yeah. In your bed. I see where that was going."

"Don't be a jerk, Eddie."

"I'm not the one with the ex in the bed," he said. "And I'm not having this argument in public. I may be Latin, but I'm not ghetto."

I stood there, my mouth agape, as he stomped down the stairs.

"Darren?" Parker's voice behind me was plaintive.

What was I supposed to do? Chase after Eddie, when he'd already said he wasn't going to argue in front of strangers? Go back to Parker, who'd caused all this trouble in the first place? Instead of doing either, I was paralyzed there, my feet on the goofy welcome mat in front of my door.

Chapter 21

El Rincón

I couldn't believe I'd been so stupid. Had Darren even broken up with Parker, as he'd said? Or was he stringing me along for the sake of his business?

My phone buzzed with a text as I walked down the sidewalk toward where I'd parked my car, and I was tempted not to answer it—to toss the phone into the trash and walk away. I didn't, though, and it was a good thing, because the text was from my father.

Meet me at El Rincón? the text read.

El Rincón was a bar on Southwest Eighth Street, also known as Calle Ocho. When Cubans of my father's generation arrived in Miami, they had clustered in that neighborhood, adjacent to downtown, and created a thriving Latin culture there. Once the Cubans had moved up the economic ladder, they'd moved west, to the ritzy neighborhood of Coral Gables and the middle-class one of Westchester.

My father had always harbored a fondness for El Rincón, and he often stopped there for a beer after work with some of the guys from his construction team. I'd been there once or twice, but never felt very at home there. Too rowdy, too macho, too un-gay.

On my way there now, I texted back to my father. If he wanted to talk to me, I was willing to meet him on ground that was familiar to him, yet away from the rest of the family.

It was rush hour, so the traffic was slow on A1A south, and I drummed my fingers on the steering wheel with impatience. A jerk on a motorcycle swerved between cars as if his trip was more important than anyone else's, and as he zoomed up behind me, I had an urge to open my door and clock him.

Of course that meant ruining my car just because I was in a bad mood, so fortunately I resisted the impulse. Eventually I was able to cut over to Alton Road, a tree-lined four-lane where traffic moved faster, though there was always the threat of a cop with a radar gun lurking around the next bend, so I couldn't pick up the speed I wanted.

For that I had to wait until I hit the causeway over to the mainland. I was able to pull a couple of zigzag stunts of my own that got me a clear path up the high bridge over Biscayne Bay, then zoom on the straightaway. Driving fast made me feel better, gave me a sense that for at least a moment I was in charge of my own forward momentum, without Phil Sweet, Darren Carter, or my father to hold me back.

It was a different world over on that side of the bay. More women, for starters, in skin-tight white pants with bare midriffs, men's dress shirts with the tails out, tank tops and T-shirts and colorful blouses bought from impoverished locals in Latin American countries, festooned with embroidery and tiny glittering bits.

I passed a young couple holding hands and wearing matching Crocs, an Arab woman in a purple hijab and baggy harem pants. Men with shoulder-length gray hair, sunglasses on their heads. Young Latinas in off-the-shoulder dresses and heavy eye makeup.

In Spanish, rincón meant corner, and El Rincón was a typical corner bar with a Latin flavor. The neon signs in the window were for Corona, Dos Equis and Polar, a Venezuelan beer with a polar bear logo. I parked a block away and walked inside, stopping by the door to let my eyes get accustomed to the gloom.

I'd expected to find my dad in the center of a group of back-slapping beer-drinking construction workers, but instead he was by himself in a booth at the back. A cluster of guys watched a soccer game from Mexico on one of the big-screen TVs, and a couple of other men sat at tables drinking. No women in the place.

I stopped at the bar and got a Polar, then slid in across from him, the bottle chilly in my hand.

"*Hola*, Papi," I said. "*¿Cómo estás?*"

"Been better." He was halfway through a Corona, and I could see where he'd been picking away at the label with his fingernail.

I didn't know how to respond to that. But he'd called this little tête-a-tête, so it was up to him to keep the conversation going.

"*Ayer*, I felt like I got hit with both barrels of a shotgun," he said after a while.

"I'm sorry if I upset you yesterday, Papi. I didn't know I was going to do it. I swear. I ...well, I spent the weekend with Darren, and he came out to his dad, and—"

"Not just you," he said. "What your abuela said about Tío Eduardo too."

"You didn't know?"

He shook his head. "I knew him in Cuba, you know. He was so *guapo, un hombre encantador*. I wanted to be like him when I grew up."

"You're pretty handsome and charming yourself."

"But I didn't want to be like him that way. And I certainly didn't want you to be."

A raucous cheer rose from the group of men watching the soccer game. When it got quiet again, I said, "I can't help who I am, Papi."

"You can't? Maybe you haven't met the right woman. When I met your mother, I knew right away she was the woman for me."

"And did you think about being with men before you met her?"

He looked horrified. "Not at all."

"Well, I've known since I was about twelve that I didn't want to meet a woman like Mami. Any woman."

I thought back for a moment to my preteen self, how confused I had been because the other boys were always gossiping about girls, who was *una chica facil*, an easy girl, and what they wanted to do to her. I was more interested when they were showing off in the showers after gym class, who had pubic hair already, how big the other boys' dicks were.

"Was it something I did to you?" my father asked, zapping me back to reality. "You were always daddy's boy. When I'd bring you to work, the other guys would call you Ramoncito, like you were a little version of me. Should I have left you with your mother instead?"

"It's nothing you did, Papi." I picked up my bottle of beer. "Most people think it's genetic, that I was born this way. Maybe some recessive gene or something that came down from abuela's parents to Tío Eduardo, through her to me."

I took a swig of my beer, and my father did too. "I know I said some bad things about maricónes," he said after a while. "I wouldn't have said them if I'd known you were..."

"I know, Papi. It's a cultural thing." I hesitated for a moment. "Do you know anyone who's gay?"

He began to shake his head, then stopped. "Señor Rosales," he said. "The one who runs the *loteria*, down at the bodega on Bird Road."

The loteria was a kind of Cuban bingo game with symbols as well as numbers. My dad would often pick up some cards at the bodega, and I'd play with him. I had only the vaguest memory of the man, tall and almost cadaverously thin.

My father looked down at the table. "We used to make fun of him, some of the workers and me, after we'd buy our tickets. He wore nail polish and makeup."

I didn't remember that. "Don't worry about me in that regard. No interest in makeup. Neither does Darren."

"Was he the one who..."

"You really want to get into this, Dad? I told you that I've known I was gay since I was twelve."

He shuddered. "No, better not to talk about it." He looked at his bottle for a moment, then at me. "You couldn't find a Cuban boy? Your mother would be happier."

I laughed. "Sorry, Papi. Love is a funny thing. What you said you felt with Mami? I felt that with Darren, back at Penn. Stupid of us to break up when we graduated. But we're back together again."

I remembered what I'd seen at Darren's apartment. Did Darren feel the same way I did? Or was I a convenient means to an end? And now that I'd come out and compared my relationship with him to the one between my parents, how could I ever take that back?

My father finished his beer, and I drained the last of mine. "I should get home," he said. "Tu mami will have dinner soon. *Venga conmigo?*"

I shook my head. I'd had enough of my family for a while, at least until I figured out what was going on between me and Darren Carter. "I've got work to do," I said.

My father stood up. "I won't say I'm happy, because I'm not. This is a hard road you're going to walk. It's not what I wanted for my son."

I resisted the urge to say that it wasn't all about him. After we parted, I resisted another urge, to go back to Darren's apartment and confront him. I had a lot of work to do, both for my ongoing business and for the joint venture, and I couldn't let all that slide.

Chapter 22

Heartless Bastard

After Eddie left, Parker kept asking me questions about Eddie and our relationship, and I had admitted that I'd gone to bed with Eddie only a short time after breaking up with Parker.

"So that's how easy it was for you?"

"We have a whole history. You know that. It's not like I met him and five minutes later I was in bed with him." I looked at him. "You want me to lie to make you feel better, Parker? Because I can."

"I think you've lied to me enough already." I figured he was angry enough to leave my apartment, but I was wrong. Instead he stalked into my bedroom and went back to sleep.

I was too upset to get much work done. I kept picking up my phone to call or text Eddie, but I'd already said what I had to say, and it was up to him to make the next move.

He didn't.

Parker woke up a couple of hours later, and I made a late dinner for both of us, and he went back to sleep. Eventually I joined him in bed, and though he reached for me, I pushed him away. I wasn't that kind of guy, despite what Eddie thought.

On Tuesday morning, I woke up first. I used the bathroom, then went out to the kitchen, where I made tea and baked some biscuits. Parker joined me in the kitchen, still wearing the same white boxer briefs.

"You can't stay here forever," I said to him. "I have work to do."

"What am I supposed to do? Go home and bury my head in the sand?"

"Don't do that. You'll find it's difficult to breathe that way."

I looked at him. "You're a wreck, Parker. You need to go home and chill. I'm not kicking you to the curb. You can call me if you need someone to talk to. But we're not together anymore, and I'm not risking my relationship with Eddie, or my business, to pretend something that I don't feel."

"You are a heartless bastard, aren't you?"

"Tell me what you really feel," I said. "Is that the way you spoke to this client of yours? He tried to be honest with you, and you lashed out at him?"

"Fuck you, Darren." He turned on his heel and stalked back to the bedroom, and about five minutes later he was dressed and on his way out the door.

"At least take a biscuit with you," I said.

"Shove the biscuit up your ass. Or up your boyfriend's ass, if that turns him on."

Then he was gone. I was certainly doing well with personal relationships, wasn't I?

I finished the whole roll of biscuits and two cups of tea, going back over every decision I'd made, wondering if I could have done something differently.

Should I have waited to go back to bed with Eddie until I was sure everything was finished with Parker? I'd been honest with Parker, ended the relationship. That made me free, didn't it?

Should I have waited for the business to take off? That was the kicker, and it probably would have been a good idea. However, Eddie had to share the blame for that decision. It wasn't like I had to pressure him into sex—he was as into it as I was.

And that boat had already left the dock, so there was no use stressing over it.

I hadn't slept well, worried that Parker might try something in the middle of the night, so I went back to bed, and by the time I woke up it was early afternoon.

I had to scramble to get to the restaurant in Aventura where I had to conduct a training. It took longer than I expected, and I ended up sticking around through the first dinner rush and doing the tea brewing myself.

Driving home, all my doubts returned. I still hadn't heard from Eddie, and I wondered if our joint venture had gone down the drain along with whatever feelings Eddie had for me. I tried to get some work done that evening, but I couldn't concentrate on advertising strategies and number-crunching, and I ended up taking a sleeping pill and zonking out.

I was still asleep when my phone rang the next morning. "Darren Carter?" a gruff male voice asked.

"Uh-huh."

"This is Detective Randall of the Miami Gardens police. We'd like you to come in this morning and answer a few questions about your friend Parker Kane. Ten o'clock suit you?"

I rolled over and looked at the clock. It was a few minutes after nine. "Yeah, I can make that. Where do I go?"

He said that he'd text me the address, and I jumped into the shower and got dressed. I didn't even have a chance to check my e-mail before I had to be out the door and in the car.

I drove up A1A for a while until I could cut across to the mainland through the high-end waterfront city of Bay Harbor Islands, then onto the Broad Causeway, a long, low old-fashioned bridge over Biscayne Bay. I rolled down the windows and let the salt air rush in, heard the honk of a boat's horn requesting the bridge go up. This was the Florida I loved, the single-family homes ringing the water, sailboats moored to my right and left, a lazy sense of happiness floating in the air.

That dissipated quickly as I kept going across 125th Street, through a mixed neighborhood of bagel bars and high-end gyms, where automobile exhaust replaced the fresh air and the angry bells of a truck reversing split the air.

Once I crossed US 1, run-down commercial buildings with signs in Haitian Creole took over. I passed an elementary school where boys and girls in T-shirts and shorts jogged slowly around the perimeter, then a day-care center where tinier kids played on a slide painted to look like a dragon.

I was still new enough to South Florida that the quick shifts in neighborhood struck me, the way towers full of wealthy people clustered along the water while a mile inland single-parent families struggled to make the rent on run-down apartments. I remembered a song from one of my favorite Broadway musicals, *Pump Boys and Dinettes*, how you didn't need a road map to know where the lines were drawn.

The GPS in my phone led me to NW Twenty-Seventh Avenue, a commercial strip lined with fried-chicken restaurants, discount shoe stores, and pharmacies that advertised they filled Obamacare prescriptions. I parked at a modern three-story building and went into the bland lobby, where I checked in with a clerk behind a bulletproof glass window and was told that Detective Randall would be with me shortly.

I sat on one of the hard plastic chairs as a heavy-set black woman argued with the clerk behind the window about the whereabouts of her son, who had been arrested on a trumped-up charge because he was a young black male. An elderly woman who was there to report a break-in at her house kept saying, "Amen," and "I hear you, sister."

It didn't bother me that I was the only white person in the room, but I wondered what the people around me thought. I didn't know much about the city of Miami Gardens, only that it was primarily African-American, that it was dominated by the Hard Rock football stadium and the Calder race track and casino. It wasn't a place where young white guys like me usually hung out.

While I waited, I pulled up the website for the college where Parker's client had gone on his rampage. It was one of the for-profit outfits that had sprung up during the years of easy financial aid like mushrooms after a spring rain. It offered a bunch of certificates and degrees in areas like website design, medical office technology, and criminal justice—the one Jarvis had been enrolled in.

I didn't know anything about Jarvis other than his name, but I resisted Googling for information about the incident because I wanted to cultivate ignorance with Detective Randall and get the hell out of there and back to my real life.

An hour later I was still waiting. When a young guy with a red do-rag finished at the window I went up and asked about Detective Randall, and I was informed that he was still busy and would get to me when he could.

"Can I reschedule?" I asked. "I have work to do."

"You'd have to talk to him."

I went back to my seat and dialed the number in my phone that Randall had used when he called me, but got his voice mail.

I tried to do some work, but I couldn't concentrate. I was too fidgety, worrying about Parker and wondering what this detective thought I could say. I wanted to call Eddie and cry on his shoulder about my problems, but from the way he'd looked when he walked out of my apartment, I doubted I'd get much sympathy.

It was nearly noon by the time the receptionist called me. She took my driver's license, snapped a photo of my face, and printed a sticker for me to wear. "Take the elevator to the third floor," she said.

Detective Randall looked like he belonged on the playing field at Hard Rock Stadium. He was a tall, beefy guy with a shaved head, wearing a black polo shirt embroidered with *Miami Gardens Police* that stretched across his chest. He'd have been a huge hit at the gay bars on South Beach.

"Thank you for coming in," he said, as he ushered me to a seat beside his desk. "Let's talk about Parker Kane. How long have you known him?"

I'd met Parker through a dating app, and I wasn't eager to get into the specifics of my personal life with this detective, but I figured it was simpler to be honest. I explained about how we'd connected online and started dating.

"He ever talk to you about his clients?"

I shook my head. "He was very professional. Even when he was obviously upset about something that had happened at work, and I asked him about it, he wouldn't tell me any details or client names."

"So he never mentioned Jarvis Dupree to you?"

"Not until Jarvis was arrested. And even then, he didn't tell me any details of his interactions with Jarvis."

"You know what happened."

"Only that Jarvis was alleged to have shot up the school where he was going, and that Parker was questioned. He was worried that you'd think he was responsible."

"That's what we're trying to establish. So he didn't tell you that Mr. Dupree had confided his intent to make the school pay for the trouble they'd caused him?"

"Not at all. Like I said, we never got into specifics, and I didn't want to look for information online about the incident because it wasn't my business."

"You're a remarkable person. Most guys would immediately jump onto Google to see what was up."

"Not so remarkable. I have my own stuff going on, and by the time this happened, I had broken up with Parker."

"Why was that?"

"Are the details of my romantic life relevant to your investigation?" I asked. "Because if they are, I'll tell you. But the way I see things right now, I'm a private citizen with no real involvement in your case."

"Just trying to understand Mr. Kane's emotional state at the time of his meetings with Mr. Dupree," Randall said. "If he was upset about his own life, and maybe not being quite as careful as he should have been with Mr. Dupree."

"I can't say anything about that. Like I said, Parker was always very professional when he spoke to me, and I never had a real sense of what kind of counseling he provided, whether he was successful or not."

Randall asked me a lot more questions, mostly the same ones slightly rephrased, but I had the same answers. I wished I could help Parker, but I didn't know how he treated his clients, and I was not going to speculate.

Randall finally let me go two hours later. I was emotionally wrung out, both because I was upset for Parker and because Randall had made me worry that by breaking up with Parker the way I had, I'd caused him to skimp on his caseload.

I was pretty sure that wasn't the case, but the doubts still niggled at me. Did I have some responsibility for the way a complete stranger had broken down and wounded a group of innocent people? What did that say about the way I led my life?

Chapter 23

Sick to My Stomach

I couldn't believe Darren was such a skank, still sleeping with that social worker even though he'd told me they'd broken up. I thought I knew him, but I realized that all my information was five years old, and I had no idea how much he'd changed during that time.

Was I the same guy I was when I marched in my cap and gown and my extended family cheered and blew air horns? I had slept with a couple of different guys in college, but committed myself to Darren for almost all of senior year. After we broke up, I went back to that previous pattern, having fun with whoever struck my fancy. I was a young, good-looking guy in New York with money in my pocket, and I spent a lot of time at gay bars, drinking and chatting and making out in back rooms and apartments.

In Miami, I had a lot less money and a lot less free time, so I'd turned to online apps. But when I met Darren again, I felt like I could stop all that, settle down with one guy, build our businesses and our lives together. It had rocked my world when I saw his ex come out of Darren's bedroom in those tight white boxer briefs.

The guy wasn't even all that good-looking—chubby face, a bit of a pot belly.

There was always a chance that Darren had been telling the truth, that I'd misconstrued what I'd seen. If that was the case, it was up to him to call or e-mail me with a better explanation. Then I'd see how I felt.

The next morning I checked my messages, but instead of hearing from Darren, I got an e-mail from the company I bought a number of herbs and spices from. *We've received word that the farm which supplies our raw ginger may have experienced an outbreak of salmonella bacteria,* it read.

My heart gave a nasty jump. I used ginger from this company in several of my simple syrups, which had been distributed to nearly two dozen bars and restaurants.

There is no evidence that the ginger we purchased and processed has been contaminated in this manner, but we are instituting a voluntary recall of all products which contain ginger harvested between the relevant dates. Please check your supplies for these UPC codes and return all unused merchandise to us for a full credit.

Well, that was just dandy.

I did some quick research and discovered that salmonella bacteria could survive on whole ginger root, as well as on dried chamomile flowers, peppermint leaves, and green tea leaves, under various storage conditions. All those were ingredients I used.

Salmonella could cause diarrhea, vomiting, abdominal pain, and fever. It could be deadly in young children, in the elderly, or those with weakened immune systems. I doubted that children or elderly people were consuming my tea-based cocktails, but I sold to a lot of gay bars, and the thought that someone with HIV could get worse from something I'd sold made me sick to my stomach.

I had supplies shipped directly to the small company that manufactured and bottled my simple syrups for me. It was a family-owned business with a warehouse and factory on the western edge of Miami-Dade County, and I debated calling the guy I dealt with.

This required an in-person visit, though. I had to know what impact this was going to have on my business as soon as possible.

I dressed and drove out along the MacArthur Causeway toward downtown, passed sailboats anchored between the causeway and the wealthy enclaves of Star and Hibiscus Island. A single catamaran left behind a gentle wake as it sailed across the expanse of sparkling water, in the shadow of a line of bay-front towers.

In front of me, an elderly man in a Rolls-Royce pulled into the turn lane for Fisher Island, where the cheapest condo cost more than four years of an Ivy League degree, and I wondered if I would ever have enough money to drive an expensive car and live in a luxurious home.

I crested the last bridge before the mainland, past the new art museum and the as-yet unfinished science museum. Cranes and new apartment towers cluttered the landscape, another sign of the way my home town was changing so rapidly around me.

There was an endless volume of traffic on the 836 expressway—a misnomer if there ever was one. I'd never been able to move in an express fashion on that road for as long as I'd been licensed to drive. The big SUV in front of me had a round decal on the back window that read *Zombie outbreak response team.* Good luck getting to the outbreak quickly in Miami traffic.

I headed north on yet another slow-moving expressway until I reached Hialeah—land of car parts stores, urgent care clinics, and karate dojos that advertised after-school programs to help with physical fitness.

The warehouse that handled my production and distribution was a low-slung building off Okeechobee Parkway, only a mile or two east of the development boundary that protected the Everglades from being overtaken with the same suburban sprawl that had infested the rest of the county.

I parked beneath the drooping brown fronds of a dying palm tree and walked inside. There was no one at the front desk, so I walked into the warehouse, lined with tall racks of metal shelving. I heard the *beep-beep* of a motorized hand truck backing up, and I followed the sound. In Spanish, I asked the driver where I could find Manny Larriaga, the guy I usually dealt with.

He directed me to the small office at the back of the room, and I darted past other hand trucks and both incoming and outgoing boxes.

Manny was about my dad's age, a heavyset guy who could have been a stunt double for Jabba the Hutt. "I got this e-mail," I said, and showed him the message on my phone.

"*¡Mierda!*" he said when he looked back up at me.

"Can you see if any of the ginger you received matches those dates and product numbers?"

He plunked away at his keyboard. "This isn't the first time we've had this problem," he said. "We started keeping detailed records a year ago to deal with it."

Manny moved so slowly that I wanted to grab the keyboard from him and search myself, but that was dumb—I had no idea how his databases were organized. Finally, he said, "Yeah, we got a shipment of ginger on the twelfth of last month that matches those codes. Used almost all of it in your products. Waiting for a new shipment any day now."

"Can we track where the affected products went?" I asked.

He nodded and generated a spreadsheet for me. He set me up in an empty office next door to his own, and I spent most of the day there, calling every bar and restaurant where the syrup had been sent, making arrangements to come by personally and pick up the product. I didn't have anything to replace it with because Manny was still waiting for that new shipment, but I promised a full refund for the syrups and replenishment as soon as possible.

Every time I made a deal like that I shuddered at the impact on my bottom line. Hell, I had no bottom line at that point—the bottom had dropped out of my business, and I'd be feeling the impact for months, as I applied credits to new deliveries that I had no money to produce.

The managers weren't happy, but they were matter-of-fact.

There had been so many product scares in the past couple of years, and this one was minor. Because they didn't keep track of which customer ordered which drink, there was no way to contact anyone who might have been affected. All I could do was pull the product back and ask the bars and restaurants to put up a discreet sign announcing the recall and asking anyone who might have suffered a reaction to contact me through my website.

I spent the rest of the afternoon into late at night traveling all over Miami-Dade and Broward counties collecting the unused bottles and dropping off the little signs.

It was nearly midnight by the time I got home and I fell into bed. In the moments before sleep overtook me, I realized that I should have called Darren and let him know about this kink in operations, but it wasn't his problem, was it? We hadn't merged yet.

Would he be worried about joining his operation with mine because of this? He couldn't be. The recall could have affected him as easily as it had me. And maybe it had. Did he get his ginger from the same place?

Would we even have a joint business if we weren't sleeping together?

I wanted to get up and call him, but I was too tired. In the morning, I had to deal with a dozen e-mails from business and individual customers, and I completely forgot about contacting Darren. The rest of the day was consumed in similar fashion, and I did little more than put out fires until I collapsed into bed.

Thursday morning I was determined to grab my life back. I woke up early and went for a long run—past all the ongoing construction along the city streets, south along Alton Road with the flow of traffic, then cutting west again to run a couple of laps around the park named after one of the dead Bee Gees. By the time I made it home I was soaked with sweat, but my body was suffused with endorphins, and after I showered and ate a power bar, I opened my laptop ready to go back to work.

The first thing that popped up was a meeting reminder. Darren and I were supposed to sit down with Phil Sweet in two hours to go over the results of our meeting in Ohio, and the way what we learned had impacted our projections.

Holy crap. We'd begun that work over the weekend at Bill's Motel and various coffee shops around Barberton, but we'd left most of the questions open-ended, and I had been so consumed with the product recall that I hadn't done any of the follow-up work. I hoped that Darren had, but once I called him I realized he hadn't either.

"Sorry, this thing with Parker spiraled out of control," he said. "I was at the police station almost all day yesterday."

"What are we going to do about this meeting?"

"What meeting?"

"The one we have with Sweet at eleven o'clock."

"That's tomorrow, Eddie."

"Nope. My calendar says Thursday. Which is today."

"Oh, my God. I totally lost track of time. We can't go talk to him without knowing what we're doing."

"I'll call and reschedule," I said.

I hung up and dialed Sweet's office. He was leaving with his wife for a sail around the Abacos, one of the less-developed chains in the Bahamas, where he'd have limited Internet access. He wanted to meet with us before he left.

Which meant that we had to get our asses in gear ASAP. I called Darren and told him to come to my place as soon as he could. "Without Parker, in case you're still baby-sitting him," I said.

"Fuck you," Darren said and hung up.

Chapter 24

Sweet Rhythm

I couldn't believe I'd gotten my days confused and hadn't done any work to prepare for the meeting with Phil Sweet. I couldn't wait for the bus, so I drove to South Beach, and all the way I kept seeing my business go down the drain.

Could I survive without Eddie's partnership and Phil Sweet's cash infusion? I didn't think so. I'd maxed out my local client base, and the money I brought in from product sales was barely enough to feed me and pay the rent. I'd been draining my meager savings, confident in the thought that Sweet's funding would carry me until I was able to get the national product distribution in place.

Then I'd met Eddie again, and all my future plans had gone into flux. Our budgets had included a minimal salary for each of us, at least in the first year. I could suck it up that long. I knew one of the managers at the specialty tea store in Aventura Mall, and I'd figured I could always pick up some shifts there if I needed extra cash. I had the tea knowledge and the customer skills, after all.

Was that my future? Keep my own business on the side and go into retail? Work my way up to a district or regional manager spot? The thought of it made me shudder. I could go back to the nonprofit world, but there was no money in that. Get another degree? In this economy it made no sense to burden myself with student loans unless I was entering a career with guaranteed earnings, but I had no head for science and a limited aptitude in business, as working with Eddie had demonstrated to me.

All in all, I was fucked. A nonmarketable college degree and what was about to be a failed business behind me. There was no way we could get together the numbers Phil Sweet wanted to see, and we were going to crash and burn. I'd walk away from there with no boyfriend and no business.

The bridge that led to Alton Road was closed for repairs so I had to continue south on A1A, past old people in new cars and the lavish yachts docked on Indian Creek Drive. Never going to have one of those. Hell, I'd be lucky to be able to keep up the payments on my used Toyota.

I got stuck behind a parade of delivery vans. Would things get any better with drone deliveries? Or would the skies simply become as crowded as the streets?

My mind was wandering, trying anything to avoid thinking of what awaited me. When Eddie answered his door, his hair was tousled, his T-shirt wrinkled, and there was a desperate look in his eyes that said he'd been having the same doubts I had.

"There's no way we can be prepared by the time of this meeting," he said. "I've been looking at what we did in Ohio, and it's nowhere near enough."

Time for me to step up. I'd let Eddie take the lead too many times in our business dealings, and he didn't look like he was in any shape to keep that up.

"Good morning to you too." I looked at my watch. "We have to be at Sweet's office in an hour, and you look like shit. Go take a shower and get dressed. Even if he shoots us down, at least we'll walk in there looking like winners."

I surprised Eddie as much as I did myself with my attitude. Somewhere in the last few blocks of my trip I must have gotten an infusion of energy. While he cleaned up, I opened my laptop and looked over the material we had. It wasn't as bad as I'd thought, but it wasn't as good as it needed to be either.

I worked on a quick PowerPoint that focused on the data that we had, avoiding what we didn't, ignoring Eddie as he came out of the shower wrapped in a towel and began to get dressed. By the time he was finished, I had something we could show Sweet. There wasn't enough time to go over it with Eddie, though.

Neither of us talked as we walked over to Sweet's office. There was too much to say, and until we finished with Sweet, we didn't know what our business future held.

"No apologies," I said, as we rode up in the elevator at his building. "We both had a lot going on this past week, but it doesn't mean we're any less dedicated or that we're going to be any less successful."

"I need to talk to you about a product recall," Eddie said, but the elevator opened, and we walked into his office. The receptionist said that he was expecting us and ushered us to his office.

"I expected you to have e-mailed me the numbers before this meeting," he said. "What's up?"

"A couple of minor snafus in the past couple of days forced us to focus on our ongoing businesses," I said, taking the lead, and trying to avoid having to go into my Parker problems. The last thing I wanted Phil Sweet to know was that I'd been interviewed by the police. "We've got a presentation to show you."

I handed him my jump drive, and he plugged it into his computer. "You'll see we've collected all the data. We just need to get the numbers crunched."

Neither of us said anything more while Sweet flipped through the screens of the presentation. Unfortunately, he was smart enough to see what was going on behind the curtain—that we hadn't done all the work he expected us to do.

Sweet looked up at us and frowned. "I expect a level of professionalism from anyone I invest with. This isn't cutting it. You guys need to seriously consider whether you can carry off this business. I'm not throwing money away on a couple of millennial slackers."

"With all due respect, neither of us are millennial slackers," Eddie said. "We're both struggling to run ongoing businesses, and we've done everything you asked so far."

He frowned. "I promised Margarita that I'd minimize my online time while we're sailing," he said. "But I want to see something from you within seven days. Or else I'm going to have to cut you loose, and we'll make arrangements for you to pay back my investment."

I gulped. We'd already spent a chunk of his cash on the trip to Ohio, and I'd been planning to use some of it for living expenses. I looked at Eddie, my eyes wide.

"We can do that," Eddie said. "Within seven days you'll have the numbers you want, and we'll prove to you that your investment in us is warranted."

Sweet stood up, and that was our cue to vamoose. Neither of us said anything until we got outside. "Well, we got our asses handed to us," Eddie said.

"What are we going to do? I can't afford to start paying him back if we fail." I was sweaty and dizzy, but I sucked it up.

"We're not going to fail," Eddie said. "But we are going to have to work as hard as we can over the next seven days." He looked at me. "Can you commit to that? Or are you still tied up with Parker?"

"I cut him loose," I said. "I feel bad about it, but I can't let him drag me down or ruin everything you and I have worked for." I looked over at him. "I'm sorry if I gave you any reason to doubt me."

He smiled and took my hand. "And I'm sorry I flew off the handle."

"So we're good again?" I asked.

"Better than good. But before we get started on numbers, I have to tell you about this ginger I've been using."

We walked down Lincoln Road in the harsh sunshine, dodging guys on roller skates, little kids playing, and people with big dogs on expandable leashes, and my heart did a couple of flip-flops as Eddie explained the consequences to his business. "Where did you buy your ginger from?" I asked, when he finished.

He told me the company, and I took a deep breath. "Thank God," I said.

He held open the door of the Starbucks for me. "What for?"

"Because I use a different supplier. I can give you some of my stock and turn you on to the guys I use."

We spent the rest of the afternoon hunched over our laptops, trading information, brainstorming ideas. "We need to cut our expenses to the bone," Eddie said after we'd crunched our numbers until they cried out for pity.

"How can we do that? We're already operating on a shoestring."

He looked at me. "We could move in together. We could save on rent that way."

My dick jumped at the idea of sleeping with Eddie every night. But could we live together? "How much are you paying?"

"Two grand a month for that lousy studio. And an extra hundred a month for parking."

"Wow. I'm only paying eleven hundred for my place." The wheels started to click in my head, despite my misgivings. "My car insurance is coming due next month, and I've been wondering how I can pay it. If you move in with me, I could sell my car and we could share yours."

"Let me call my landlord and see how fast I can get out of my lease," Eddie said.

While he made the call, I looked up the value of my old Toyota. I'd bought it used, with low mileage, and despite driving all the way from Portland to Miami, it was still in good condition, and I could get about eight grand for it. If Eddie shared the rent on my place, and I didn't have to pay for insurance or maintenance, I'd be able to cut my expenses by a big chunk.

He hung up. "Good news. He has a cousin who wants to use the place, and he's happy to let me out right away."

"So we're going to do this."

"And you're over Parker House Rolls?"

"I am. I can't completely cut him off while he's in trouble, but there's nothing romantic there."

"Then it makes sense, doesn't it?" Eddie asked. "Not just financially. But for us."

"For us," I said, and I raised my empty teacup so that he could clink his against it.

"For us," he echoed.

We left the coffee shop a few minutes later and walked west along Lincoln Road, stopping along the way at a liquor store to pick up a couple of empty boxes. I fixed us some quick pasta while Eddie began packing his liquor and his supplies, and we ferried stuff down to my car, and his.

By ten o'clock we had both cars loaded, and all Eddie had to do was pack up his clothes and his toiletries. He was sprawled on the sofa, and I sat on the floor, my back against the wall.

"I'm too beat to consider driving everything up to your place tonight," Eddie said, after he yawned. "Want to stay here with me?"

"I think I could manage that," I said, smiling. "As long as there's something in it for me."

"How about my dick in your ass?"

My dick began to stiffen in my slacks, and my ass cheeks clenched. "I hope you're going to make out with me first. I don't give up my ass so easily."

"Of course you do," Eddie said. "But making out is good."

He reached his arms out. "Come here, you."

I got up and joined him on the sofa, and leaned in for a deep kiss. Eddie smelled so good, that unique mix of musk and the memory of his bay rum cologne, and I opened my mouth to him so that our tongues could duel.

As we kissed he undid a couple of buttons of my shirt so that he could reach inside and tweak my nipples, and my body reacted with an electric surge. My dick was stiff, pressing against the fabric, and I had to reach down and adjust myself. "Are you hard for me, baby?"

Eddie whispered. He moved down to lick and kiss my neck, and I arched my back to give him access.

"Always," I murmured.

He undid the rest of my shirt buttons, and I shucked the shirt, and he began to lick his way down my chest. I groaned with pleasure as he palmed my dick through my pants. "Oh, yeah, baby," he said, his nose against my stomach.

He fumbled my pants open, and my dick popped out around the edge of the bright orange fundoshi I was wearing. "This Japanese jock strap of yours really turns me on," he said, as he hooked his fingers under the waistband and began to undo the cord that wrapped around it.

At the same time he leaned down and took my dick in his mouth, and I felt as if I'd died and gone to heaven. He gave up trying to untie the cord and instead stuck his fingers under the strap that ran along my ass crack. I was writhing in pleasure, but I knew that if I let it go on too long, I'd come in his mouth.

I gently pushed him aside and stood up. I dropped my trousers and quickly undid the fundoshi, then let it fall to the ground. I stood there naked in front of Eddie as if I was offering myself to him, nothing hidden and no holds barred.

"Like what you see?" I asked.

"Always."

"Then why the fuck are you still wearing clothes?"

"Bossy bottom," Eddie said with a laugh. As he stood up, I walked over to his bed and got onto all fours, presenting my ass to him. I heard the sounds of zippers and buttons and clothing hitting the floor, and he was there at my ass, his tongue finding its way into my hole. I shivered with pleasure.

He took his time, licking and sucking the tender flesh around my opening until I was loose and hungry for his dick. The cold squirt of lube, warmed up as Eddie circled around my pucker with his finger, then began to penetrate me with slow, deep strokes.

I began to whimper, and Eddie took that as his cue to bring his dick up to me and nose it around my hole. "Give it to me, baby," I said. "Please. I need you now."

"You are so hot," he said. His dick pushed against me, and I took a couple of deep breaths, doing my best to relax. After a brief moment of pain, I felt him inside me and the endorphins began to rise.

He balanced himself on one arm, and used his free hand to reach around and fist my dick. "Oh, yeah," I said.

"You and me, mi amor," he said, as he pushed deep into me. "Always you and me."

I pushed back at him, swallowing his dick up to the root so that his pubic hairs scraped against my ass cheeks. We moved into a sweet rhythm, push and pull, and both of us were swearing and moaning. He banged against my prostate over and over again, sending waves of pleasure through me until I couldn't stand it anymore. "I'm gonna," I panted.

"*Oye, guapo,* come for me." The Spanish turned me on even more, and as he jerked me harder and harder, I exploded, sending off fireworks inside my body. I clenched my ass around his dick, and he pushed in and out a couple of times, then shot off. He stayed inside me for a moment, both of us panting with exertion, until he pulled out and we collapsed together on the bed.

"Going to have to wash these sheets in the morning," he mumbled, and he was out.

I stayed awake for another couple of minutes, thinking about what the next day held. We still had so much to do to prepare for Phil Sweet, and we'd have to clear out of Eddie's place and get him settled at mine. Sell my car, keep both our businesses going, handle the fallout from the ginger recall and Parker's problems.

Could we manage it all? In the afterglow of sex, everything seemed possible—but would it feel the same way in the harsh morning light?

Chapter 25

Left Hand, Right Hand

The next few days went by so fast I felt dizzy whenever I stopped to consider how much we'd accomplished. Darren helped me move all my crap up to his apartment, and we mapped out our strategy for the next few days. We both had existing clients to handle as well as all the work we had to do for Phil Sweet.

The warehouse in Hialeah got in a fresh shipment of ginger and began manufacturing new product for me. Darren sold his car, and we set up a schedule for using mine to make deliveries and handle customer issues. We both called a moratorium on looking for new business, at least until we'd made our presentation to Sweet and seen where we stood.

The one thing I made time for was dinner at my parents' house on Sunday. I'd promised my mother to bring Darren, and before we left for Westchester I prepped him. "Try not to be too gay," I said. "It's hard enough for my parents to accept that I like guys."

"So no sex talk? How I love it when you speak Spanish to me as you plow my ass?"

"Darren."

He held up his hands. "No worries. I'll be as straight as I can be."

"Which is not very," I grumbled.

"You think I'm that much of a flamer? Remember, my father had no idea I was gay."

"Parents are weird. They see what they want to see." I looked over at him. "And no, I don't think you're that much of a flamer. It's just, the whole tea thing, the more I think about it, the gayer it seems."

Darren crossed his arms over his chest. "There is nothing gay about tea."

"Oh come on. The mincing around during the Japanese tea ceremony? And even my business is pretty frou-frou when you think about it. My parents have never had anything to drink more adventurous than a Cuba libre or a mojito."

"We ought to turn them on to what we make," Darren said. "Seriously. You know what your mother cooks, right? What cocktail would you serve with Cuban food?"

I did sell some mixers to a Cuban cigar bar on Lincoln Road, heavy on the flavors of rum and coconut, but they were too sweet to serve as pre-dinner cocktails. "Maybe a citrus and white tea mix with gin," I said. "That's bright and simple, and it could be a good aperitif."

"There you go. And maybe my coconut and green tea mix for after dinner? Something sweet but with a tang?"

I pulled out a bottle of my citrus simple syrup and a bottle of gin, and Darren prepared a half-dozen packets of tea. I was on edge as we drove out to Westchester.

"I've been in Miami for six months, and I've never been out this way before," Darren said, as he peered through the windshield as if we were touring a foreign country. Which for him I guess we were.

"So many of the signs on businesses are in Spanish," he said. "Do people out here not speak English?"

I felt a momentary surge of resentment, but I swallowed it. "The older people don't speak so well," I said. "And the recent immigrants. Most everyone else is bilingual. The signs are more a cultural thing, I think."

"And your family speaks English, right?"

"My parents both grew up here," I said. "They went to American schools. My father, especially, wanted to make sure that Connie and I spoke perfect English, and he used to correct me all the time. Any time I said 'um' he'd start to chant like some Tibetan monk. Ummm....ummm."

Darren laughed.

"My mom was the one who was determined that we be bilingual, and we used to speak Spanish to our grandparents too. And of course in school most of our friends were Cuban or South American and we'd speak Spanglish to them."

"I envy you," Darren said, as I turned off Coral Way and into the neighborhood where I'd grown up. "Having a close family, living in the place where you grew up. It must give you a real sense of centeredness."

I'd never thought about it that way. "Sometimes it's almost suffocating," I said. "If I run into someone I knew in high school, I worry about having to come out to them. As soon as I say that I'm living on South Beach, it's like they look at me differently. All my old friends are either living at home or married, and they all have regular jobs like at banks or restaurants. Nobody gets being an entrepreneur, living on my own."

I parked on the swale in front of my parents' house and wondered what Darren would think of it. The exterior paint had faded to a pale pink and the lawn was patchy. It was a single-story building with an orange barrel-tile roof like every other one on the block, nothing fancy, but I knew how hard my parents had worked to be able to afford it.

The front door opened, and my mother stepped out. I took a deep breath. "You ready for this?" I asked Darren.

"With you all the way," he said, and he squeezed my hand.

I introduced him to my mother, and she insisted on kissing his cheek and hugging him. "I'm so pleased to meet you." She took his hand. "Come inside and meet my husband and my mother-in-law."

I trailed behind them, the prodigal son forgotten for the moment. My father was more formal, shaking Darren's hand, and Darren leaned down to kiss my grandmother on her cheek as she sat like a queen in the recliner chair in the living room.

"Where's Connie?" I asked.

"She's bringing her *novio*," my mother said. She turned to Darren. "Sorry, that means boyfriend in Spanish."

"We brought some of the stuff we sell for you guys to taste," I said. "I'm starting you out with a cocktail, okay?"

I escaped to the kitchen with the bag of liquor and mixers I'd bought, leaving Darren to get acquainted with my parents and my abuela. By the time I had the drinks prepared, Connie had arrived with her boyfriend, and I brought a tray of cocktails out to the living room as she introduced him.

He was a wiry guy in his late twenties, close to six feet, with close-cropped blond hair and sharp planes in his face. Not my type at all, but I could see how Connie would find him handsome. "This is Kyle," she said. He wore a white guayabera, and I wondered if that was something Connie had suggested.

She introduced everyone to him, stopping at Darren, who jumped into the breach. "Darren Carter. I'm Eddie's novio."

I was impressed that he got the pronunciation right, though I freaked at the blatant statement.

He shook hands with Kyle and kissed Connie's cheek. "I'm Eddie," I said. "And I'll be your bartender this evening. Who wants to try a cocktail?"

Connie had brought a *tres leches* cake from my father's favorite bakery for dessert, and as she took it into the kitchen, I passed the drinks around, explaining about the mix of gin with green and white tea.

"What's the difference between green and white?" Connie asked when she returned. "Besides the color, I mean."

"It's all the same plant," I said. "Camellia sinensis. The white tea comes from leaves that are picked during a few days in early spring.

It's steamed rapidly and then dried. Green tea is picked later in the season, and it's partially fermented. So the flavor profile is different."

"I don't know," my father said, sniffing the drink suspiciously. "Tea with gin?"

Abuela had no hesitation. She took a big gulp. "*Deliciso*," she said. "Go on, Ramon, try it."

My father took a tentative sip, and his eyebrows raised. "It's good," he said. *Refrescante*." He stumbled to add, "Refreshing," for the benefit of the Americanos in the room.

Everyone agreed with him, and we sipped for a moment. Then my mother turned to Kyle. "What do you do for work, mi amor?"

"Nuclear medicine tech at Jackson," he said, naming the big public hospital in Miami. "I went to USF and majored in biology, because my parents wanted me to go to medical school. But I couldn't face that much extra studying, so I went to the community college over on the west coast to be a technologist. It's good money, and I like the work."

My mother nodded with pleasure. I could see her already getting Connie set up in a house nearby, ready to pump out babies.

"What's your last name?" I asked, hoping it would be something vaguely Latin, for Connie's sake.

"Shevchenko," he said.

"What kind of name is that?" my father asked.

"All of my grandparents came from Ukraine," he said. "I was born in New Hampshire, but we moved to Tampa when I was a kid. Most of my friends were Cuban-American so I learned a lot of Spanish slang." He looked embarrassed. "Most of it can't be repeated in polite company, though."

Everyone laughed, and soon enough we went into the dining room for dinner. As we ate, Abuela kept asking Kyle medical questions, as if he was a doctor. She had been having acid reflux, and her doctor had prescribed a medication. What did he think of it?

I was impressed that he was able to answer so knowledgeably, easily admitting when he didn't know the answer to a question. And I was also pleased that the attention had shifted to him and Connie instead of me and Darren.

It was Darren's turn to shine once dinner was finished. "When I lived in Portland, I worked at a museum," he said. "My boss used to take wealthy donors out to fancy restaurants and sometimes I got to go along, to explain what our collection needed and what we hoped to do with the funds."

Everyone nodded politely.

"We'd have this terrific meal, and when I asked for tea, they'd bring out a very standard selection—little bags of Earl Grey, English breakfast, and so on. Nothing unique or interesting, and the servers had no idea what tea could complement what we'd had for dinner, or what we'd ordered for dessert."

"Darren is a tea aficionado," I said. "Back when we were at Penn, he turned me on to all the different varieties of tea."

"So I got this idea," Darren continued. "I sat down with a friend who was a chef and started making up different blends of teas with herbs and spices. Something unique, and a beverage that would add something special to the meal."

I stood up. "Why don't I clear the table while Darren brews up some tea for us."

My mother tried to protest. "No, you sit with Connie and Kyle," I said. "Let us wait on you for a change."

I began rinsing dishes and loading the dishwasher as Darren put a pot of water on to boil. "This is going well, isn't it?" he asked in a low voice.

"My parents were always polite when I brought friends home in high school," I said. "It was only afterward that they'd say what they really felt. That a girl was homely, or a boy was dumb. '*Borra con el codo lo que escribe con la mano*.' His left hand doesn't know what his right hand is doing."

"You think they'll say something like that about me?"

"Depends on how much they like the tea."

He looked at me, and I could see the fear in his eyes. "Don't worry. I'm sure they'll like it. And you. After all, I like you, and I have good taste."

He rolled his eyes, then concentrated on pouring the tea. I got the cake Connie had brought from the refrigerator and carried it to the dining room. *Tres leches* means three milks, and it was a traditional Nicaraguan dessert—a sponge cake soaked in evaporated milk, condensed milk, and heavy cream. Rich and overly sweet, and I hoped Darren's tea would balance it well.

He explained what everyone was drinking as he brought the cups to the table. "Wow, I never knew tea could taste like this," Kyle said, after he'd taken a sip.

"You probably only know the generic tea you can buy at the grocery," Darren said.

"How do you come up with these?" my mother asked, and she and Darren talked about recipes and tasting. She'd learned to cook by watching her mother and her grandmother, adding a pinch of this and a dollop of that, and she understood his approach perfectly.

I stole a glance at my father as they talked. He was eating his square of white cake with creamy white icing, not saying anything. It had to be a lot to throw at him at once—his son and his daughter both dating Americanos. Both male. Not the way he'd expected things to turn out.

But I'd never expected to reconnect with Darren Carter, or end up in business with him. And who knew how that story would play out, once we had our numbers together for Phil Sweet.

Chapter 26

Keep Running

I thought the dinner with Eddie's family went well, though he looked like he was waiting grimly to hear complaints from his parents. On our way home that evening he was in a bad mood.

"You didn't need to throw those Spanish words in," he said. "My family speaks English, you know."

"I was trying to be nice." I looked over at him. "Are you angry I said I was your novio?"

"You don't know what those words mean," he said.

"It was pretty clear. Are you saying our relationship isn't the same as Connie's with her boyfriend?"

"You didn't need to throw it up in their faces like that."

"Are you embarrassed by me? Was I too gay for you? Because you've never minded when I'm sucking your dick."

"Don't be an asshole."

"Then don't think about putting your dick in my asshole."

He gripped the steering wheel and glared ahead. "Maybe this isn't going to work out," he said.

"What? You and me together? Our business?"

I couldn't believe he was being so obnoxious. Maybe I didn't know him as well as I thought I did. "You want to move back to your apartment? Forget about this deal with Sweet?"

"I can't go back there. My landlord already moved his cousin in."

"What do you want to do, Eddie?"

He groaned. "I know. I'm being a jerk. I'm sorry. This whole thing with my parents has me freaked out."

"I don't understand why. They were nice to me. And I loved hearing your grandmother talk about her brother, how handsome and charming he was, so much like you."

"And didn't you see the way my father was grimacing that whole time? He idolized his uncle and only discovered that his uncle was gay last week. The same time I came out to him."

"You think he's angry?"

"I think he feels like he's been lied to his whole life. Wouldn't you feel that way?"

"I don't know. I never met my dad's parents, and my mom didn't get along with her parents so I hardly ever saw them. I don't have the close family you do." I took a deep breath. "But I wish I did."

"They did seem to like you," he admitted.

"And they love you. It'll work out eventually."

"I wish I could believe that."

We were both too wiped out to do much work that night, and there was still a difficult undercurrent between us, so we stayed on our respective sides of the bed. I did wake up to find Eddie curled against me, which would have been sweet if he hadn't pulled away as soon as he realized.

The next couple of days were awkward. We were both trying to stay out of each other's way, though it seemed like anything I did set Eddie off. "Do you have to leave so much dirty crap in the sink?" he asked one day.

"I'm in the middle of blending," I said, looking up at him. I'd been drying chamomile in the oven and reducing a lavender-infused simple syrup on the stove, and there were pots and trays in the sink. I wasn't going to stop in the middle of what I was doing to wash up.

"You're always in the middle of something."

I was about to ask what he meant by that, but I backed off. I didn't want to escalate a minor argument into World War Three.

But I did worry that we weren't going to be able to carry on this way much longer. It had clearly been a mistake to move in together so quickly, and into such a small apartment. We should have found other ways to save money and retain our independence.

What was done was done, though. Once we had the next jolt of cash from Phil Sweet, maybe we'd talk about moving—either separately, or together into a bigger place so we weren't always in each other's back pocket.

Phil had e-mailed us that he'd be in a resort called Treasure Cay in the Abacos, where they had a strong Wi-Fi signal, and he set up a video call with us. Eddie and I worked late into the night the day before the call, going over our numbers again and again, brainstorming problems and opportunities.

His laptop had the better camera so we set it up on the kitchen table, logged into Skype, and placed the call. When Phil showed up on the screen he looked tan and rested, and I felt a momentary pang of jealousy that we'd been working our butts off while he was taking it easy.

It was a foolish thought. I was sure he'd worked just as hard in Silicon Valley, at the expense of his first marriage and his family. "Hey, Phil," I said.

"Hi, Phil," Eddie echoed. "We've been working those numbers you wanted, and we've got a dynamite proposal for you. We've even come up with some packaging ideas that will work for both the liquid cocktail line and the packaged teas."

"That's going to be a problem," Phil said. "I'm not sure there is going to be a joint product line after all. A buddy of mine on the West Coast told me that Teavana has a big move in the works to expand into the consumer tea market with the same kind of mixes that Darren's been planning."

My heart skipped a beat, but I said, with more confidence than I felt, "Those rumors have been going around for a while. Big companies move like molasses, Phil. You know that. We can be more nimble and get to the market first."

"Even if you did, there's no way you can compete with a company like that on advertising and shelf space. I'm afraid the packaged teas are going to be a no-go for me."

I sat back, my mouth open. My whole business was going down the drain because some executive in Seattle had seen the same market opportunity I had?

Eddie leaned forward. "What about my part of the business?" he asked. "Originally you said that the cocktail part wasn't strong enough to work on its own. But I've been running a lot of numbers and the margins are much higher than I expected. My part would have been carrying Darren's anyway."

"I see that," Sweet said. "Good job on those projections. What I want you to do is reconfigure things to remove the packaged tea part and see how it looks. Get back to me when you have that done."

He ended the call, and the screen went dark.

"You've been planning to cut me out of this business all along, haven't you?" I demanded of Eddie.

"It's all in the numbers, Darren," he said. "Retail markup is so much less in packaged goods like tea than it is in cocktail components. I was never planning to shut you out, but I had to do what I could to salvage the business."

"For yourself."

"For us. We can still work together. You have the tea knowledge and a great palate. I can handle the production and finances. We'll work together on marketing."

I couldn't hear anything else he said. All I knew was that he'd been aware that my business was doomed, and he hadn't said anything. I was having trouble breathing, and I needed to get out of there.

I stood up and pushed my chair back so hard it fell backward on the floor. "I need to go for a run."

"I'll come with you."

"I want to be on my own."

I stumbled into my running clothes, and when I came out of the bedroom Eddie stood up. "Please, Darren," he said. "I wasn't trying to cut you out."

"I don't know that."

I pushed past him, out into the hallway. I ran down the stairs and outside, and took off as fast as I could for the beach. I hardly noticed the landscape changing until I got across Collins Avenue and a narrow rectangle of bright blue-green ocean appeared before me, framed by sea grape hedges on each side of the brick path. Something began to open up inside me when I saw that, and I hurried forward, then turned right down the path that ran alongside the beach.

A mix of high and low apartment towers loomed ahead of me to the right, and as I ran, I got occasional glimpses of the ocean to my left. I focused on the thud of my feet on the bricks, the light saltwater breeze, the occasional sounds of motorcycles, trucks, and emergency sirens on A1A.

Why had I ever decided to take a chance on such a flighty business? Eddie was right. The whole tea thing was so gay, and the way I'd configured things it wasn't enough to support a real business. Hell, I'd been having trouble supporting myself, and though I'd been trying to ignore the fact, he was right—the cocktail revenues were going to carry the packaged tea business.

Had he kept going with me because he knew my business meant something to me? Why hadn't we talked about what those numbers meant earlier, before Phil Sweet dropped his bombshell on us?

It was clear there was no good business model that would support the way I'd hoped to expand my business. And the last few months had shown me that I couldn't keep living on a shoestring, depleting my meager savings. There was going to be no saving Tea by D.

What did that mean for my relationship with Eddie, though? Would we keep living together if we weren't business partners anymore? Was there a way we could keep working together, or was he blowing smoke up my ass?

I was drenched in sweat, and my legs began to ache, but I kept running.

Chapter 27

Cuban Curses

I couldn't believe Darren ran out on me, right at the time we needed to talk. He was such a flake.

I'd known that back in college. Him with his silly tea rituals, the tiny Japanese cups, the insistence on timing how long the water boiled. I'd accepted it all because I was horny for him. I had been too focused on sex to realize that Darren had some serious communication issues, starting with his father. He didn't want to talk, so I took my cues from him and didn't say what was on my mind either.

My brain told me that my business could be leaner and stronger without Darren. Yeah, he had a better palate than I did, and way more tea knowledge. But I could always hire that out, right? I was the guy with the head for numbers, the one who could manage production and distribution. What did I need him for anyway? Especially if he was going to run away at the first sign of trouble.

When I heard Darren's cell phone ring, I realized that he had left it behind when he went out to run. I checked the display and saw the call was from Parker.

Another reason to jettison our relationship. He was still caught up with his ex and with his ex's drama.

I shook my head and went back to the numbers, starting to cut out everything that related to the packaged goods business. It was complicated because we'd amortized product development across both lines and assumed that Darren would handle that aspect as part of his regular salary.

It took an hour at a time to redo the numbers with a different amortization schedule, and every time I saw his initials next to a task I got more irritated with Darren. Look at how much work he'd left me with! Even though this was going to be my business now, and it was up to me to put in the work, I was still annoyed that he wasn't there to help.

When Darren finally came back in, he looked worn-out. "Parker called," I said, handing him the phone.

"Did you talk to him?"

"Nope. Just saw his name on the display."

He grabbed the phone and stalked into the bedroom. I watched the way his sweaty nylon shorts gripped his ass, and swallowed hard. No more of that for me. I was taking a vow of celibacy until I had made a success of my business. What I should have done from the start. Even if Phil Sweet had wanted us to work together, I should have resisted getting sexy with Darren again. I should have known where it was going to lead.

And yet, as I worked the numbers I couldn't bring myself to remove Darren completely from the equation. I left in a salary for him as well as the responsibility for product development and quality. I pushed myself to finish because I wanted to have something to talk to him about when he was cleaned up and ready to get back to work.

But when he finally came out of the bedroom he was fully dressed and carrying a backpack. "Parker's in more trouble," he said. "I have to go over there. I think I'm going to stay there for a day or two."

My mouth opened in surprise. "You're walking out now? When we have so much to figure out?"

"There's nothing for me to figure," he said. "I'm out of the picture."

He grabbed his phone, and I heard him muttering as he summoned an Uber. And then he walked out.

I stared at the closed door. Had he just ditched not only me, but the business he'd worked to start? Sure, things were going to have to change, but I had made a place for him, hadn't I? Which he would have seen if he'd taken five minutes to talk to me instead of hurrying over to hold Parker House Rolls' hand.

There was that problem he had with communication again. How were we going to change that? Darren had taken the first step, by recognizing that he'd shut out his father, and trying to reconnect. And we'd certainly talked a lot more in the last few weeks than we had in the year we'd dated in college, when all we were concerned about was jumping into bed together.

But now he'd done the same thing again—run out without talking to me.

I started muttering the Cuban curses I had heard my father use when he hit his thumb with a hammer as he was fixing something that Connie or I had broken. I couldn't believe I remembered so many of them, or how appropriate they all were. *Coño, cabrajo, comemierda, hijo de puta, cabron, bugarrón, comepinga.* The fact that the last two were derogatory toward gay men only made them that much more relevant.

I'd hated hearing those words come out of my father's mouth when I was a teenager and beginning to realize that I was something he despised—a butt-fucker, a dick-sucker. A maricón, a faggot. A mariposa, the same word used for butterfly.

I'd never considered I could come out to my family. I'd gone to college in Philadelphia instead of staying in Florida, even though I had been offered a full scholarship to both UF and FSU, and going to

Penn required student loans and work-study. I needed that distance from my family to figure out who I was.

I'd moved to New York after graduation instead of returning to Miami because I knew what I liked to do in bed, and knew that wouldn't go over well in the macho Latin culture of my hometown.

And now here I was, back in South Florida, out and proud. I'd gone back into the closet as soon as I stepped off that plane at Miami International, with no plans to ever come out to my family. And yet, after only a couple of weeks back together with Darren, I'd pushed open that door forever.

My father still didn't seem happy about my announcement, and I worried that things might never be the same between us. I'd given up a closeness with him in favor of one with Darren, and now Darren was gone.

I sighed. There was nothing to do but go back to work. I spent the rest of the day working and reworking those numbers, and though they looked stronger without the packaged tea business, I got no pleasure in seeing that. Instead I only felt empty.

What was I going to do? I couldn't stay at Darren's apartment anymore if we weren't together. Did I want to move back in with my parents to save money? But I'd have to tell them that I'd broken up with Darren, so quickly after introducing him. That would make me look like a flake, wouldn't it? Like I couldn't keep anything together.

It all hinged on what Phil Sweet would say to the new set of numbers. Would I be able to convince him that the cocktail business was solid enough? If I couldn't, then I'd be right back where I was when all this started, trying to make my entrepreneurial efforts profitable enough to support me. And I'd already seen how hard that was.

Damn Darren Carter, anyway. I'd been fine on my own before he horned into the picture. I'd had a lot of fun hanging out at bars pushing my cocktail mixes, and lots of casual sex that kept my dick in a constant state of erection.

Something had been missing, though. Something I hadn't realized I had lost until I ran into Darren at Sweet's office.

I looked at the clock. Was it cocktail hour yet? Because I sure as hell needed a drink. It was four-thirty, the time my father might be at El Rincon, hefting his one after-work beer in the company of his coworkers and friends. On impulse, I picked up my phone and pressed the speed dial for his cell.

"Hola, Papi," I said when he answered. Behind him I heard Celia Cruz on the sound system at the bar, singing *Oye Como Va*—hey, how's it going. "You going to be at El Rincon for a while?"

"You want to come over here? I'll wait for you."

I said I'd head over right away, and five minutes later I was in my car heading toward the mainland. What was I going to see him for? I didn't know why, but I needed to talk to him.

All the way across Miami, the setting sun glaring into my windshield, I went over what I would say. My business was failing? My relationship was over? Could he put his arm around my shoulders and promise me everything would be okay, the way he had when I was a boy? "*Todo estará bien*," he'd say, when I'd done poorly on a test at school. When I broke my ankle roller-blading. When I was cut from the soccer team because I wasn't fast enough.

I parked in the lot beside my father's truck and walked inside. Celia Cruz had been replaced by Willy Chirino singing "*Tu Eres Mejor*," from his *Afrodisiac* album, which I'd listened to over and over again when I was a teenager. "My friends ask what have you done to me?" Chirino sang in Spanish. It was a song about how love had changed him, and back then, I'd longed to feel that emotion.

Now that I had, it wasn't so great.

I found my father by the bar, and he hugged me. "*Mi hijo todo crecido*," he said, to his friends, though I didn't feel all grown up at that point. He ordered me a beer, and we moved to a booth at the back of the bar.

"You look sad, mi hijo," he said. "So you come to your papi to cheer you up?"

I nodded. "Trouble with the business." I explained in a rush about Teavana, and Phil's suggestion that we drop our plan to take Darren's packaged tea business into the grocery aisle.

"And Darren?" my father asked, when I was finished. "What does he think of this?"

"He got mad and walked out."

My father shook his head. "Not good in a business partner," he said. "You are still, you know, together?"

"I don't know, Papi. I don't know anything anymore."

"Of course you do, mi hijo. You are a smart boy. You always have been, ever since you first started to talk, earlier than anyone else's baby. And all those good grades you brought home! Tu mami and I were so proud of you. The smartest in your class. The college scholarships. So many accomplishments!"

"But what if that's all in the past, and everything was just possibility, potential? Now I'm just a failure."

"You don't speak like that," my father said. "Not of my brilliant son, my Eduardito. I will not hear it."

His grin was broad. "Now, drink up, okay? Tu mami will expect us home for dinner soon. I hear she is making mojo pork tonight. Your favorite!"

"No, that's Connie's favorite," I said. "Mine is Moros y Cristianos."

"Then you will be happy for your sister." He leaned in close to me. "What do you think of this Kyle?" he asked. "Will he be good to her?"

I thought of the way Kyle looked at Connie, the warmth and affection and zing of energy that passed between them. It was the same way I felt about Darren—and look how that was working out.

"I'll take it under advisement," I said. That was a phrase one of my father's bosses had often used, and my father had appropriated it for himself. It seemed a good summary of what was going on with me and Darren as well.

Chapter 28

Tests

"They had no grounds to fire me," Parker said as I walked in the door of his apartment. "I didn't do anything wrong. So they just said they're reorganizing. Bastards."

His hair was lank, and a scruffy beard was beginning to form on his chin. "Can you get unemployment?" I asked.

"I guess so. But I haven't done anything about it."

"Well, you need to. That shit takes time."

He sat down on his ratty sofa, hard, and began to cry. "I don't know what to do."

"Get a grip, Parker. You lost your job. It's not the worst thing in the world. Are the police still questioning you?"

"I talked to that detective yesterday, but he wouldn't say anything."

I blew out a long breath. "First things first. Go take a shower and get cleaned up." I realized that was what I'd said to Eddie when I found him despairing too. What was that all about? "While you do that, I'll look into the unemployment thing."

I liked having something to do that took my mind off Eddie, our failed relationship, and the way I'd been removed from my own business. I opened my laptop, logged onto Parker's Wi-Fi router, and went to the website for the state of Florida's unemployment insurance benefits.

Once I was at the right place, I left that window in the background and opened a new one, searching for anything in the news about Jarvis Dupree. All I could find was that he was still in police custody.

By the time Parker came out of the shower, his hair wet and a towel wrapped around his waist, I had almost forgotten about the tea business. "Come over here and let's get you registered for unemployment," I said.

Parker crossed the room and dropped his towel to the floor. His long, slim dick was hard, curving slightly at the end like a crescent moon. I'd enjoyed blowing him many times, and I was so tempted to grab his ass and pull him close to me, swallow him and suck all my problems away.

But that wasn't going to solve anything, and would most likely make everything worse. "Go back in your bedroom and put some clothes on."

"You don't care about me anymore?" Parker said plaintively.

"Of course I do. If I didn't, I wouldn't be here." I made some shooing motions. "Put that thing away and get focused."

He stalked back to the bedroom, leaving the towel on the floor, and I couldn't help watching the smooth globes of his ass bounce slightly as he walked. What would it hurt to jump his bones again? We were both going through a bad time. We could comfort each other.

But it still felt wrong. I was done with Eddie, both in business and personally, but that didn't mean it was a good idea to jump back into bed with Parker House Rolls.

Shit. I was even calling him by Eddie's nickname.

He came out of the bedroom in a loose pair of nylon shorts, making it evident that he was still hard. I made him sit down next to me and walked him through registering for unemployment. Every time I leaned over close to him I smelled his lavender soap, his coconut shampoo, and my dick was unrelentingly hard.

"There," Parker said, when he clicked the final Submit button. "I did what you wanted. Can I get a reward now?"

"What are you, a performing dog?"

He put his hands up in front of him like paws, and panted with his tongue out. I patted the top of his head and said, "Good boy."

He frowned. "Not the reward I was hoping for."

"All you're going to get. Now show me your résumé."

"I don't have one. Last time I looked for a job I just filled out online forms."

I groaned. "You're a big pot of problems, aren't you, Parker?"

I opened up a résumé template in Word, and dragged out the details of Parker's education and his work experience. "What did you do during this time here?" I asked, pointing to a gap of almost a year between his first and second jobs in social work.

"I kind of had a substance-abuse problem."

"You never said anything about that to me."

"It wasn't something I wanted to put in my dating profile."

I stared at him, and it took him a minute or two to give in. "That first job sucked," he said. "I was only hourly, part-time, working at this AIDS counseling center in Little Haiti. You know what it's like talking to people every day who have this potentially fatal disease but don't want to face up to it?"

I didn't. My first job back in the States after my year in Japan was at the Asian art museum in Portland. Part-time, hourly, like Parker's, only I spent my days researching and cataloging donated art works, immersed in things like Meiji-era porcelain. I didn't know anyone who was HIV positive—or at least no one who told me that he was. I read the articles in the gay press about PrEP, the pre-exposure prophylaxis for HIV, but I wasn't that active and when I did anything, I was very careful. To me, AIDS was a disease of the past.

"That must have been tough," I said.

"It was. But I was so enthusiastic, you know, every day I'd come to work ready to talk about condoms and drug regimens, and I could see I wasn't making any difference. Then the agency lost a big funding source and cut me loose. I started hanging out in bars, and I ran into one of the guys I'd counseled there. He turned me on to molly, and for the next few months that's all I did—get high and have sex."

I was angry. Such an important piece of information, and Parker had withheld it from me. I'd thought he was a sweet, shy guy without a lot of sexual experience, and here he'd been lying to me all along.

Kind of like Eddie Gonzalez. He hadn't told me about the jobs he was applying for on Wall Street. But I hadn't told him about Japan either. So call that a wash.

This latest betrayal, though, that hurt. How long had he known that my part of the business wasn't viable? Before he moved in to my apartment—where he still was?

"You don't hate me, do you?" Parker said in a small voice, and I realized I'd forgotten all about him.

"No, of course not," I said. "You're human, just like everybody else. How did you pick yourself up after that?"

"I ran into a friend of mine from social work school, and he told me about the place he was working. I applied for a job there, and I had to take a drug test." He wiped a couple of tears from his eyes. "That was a wakeup call for me. I realized I was never going to get anywhere until I was clean. I waited a couple of days to schedule the test and drank one of those detox drinks, and I was able to pass the test and get the job."

"That's awesome. You didn't keep using, did you?"

He shook his head. "No. Once I had the job, I didn't want to risk losing it. I got a couple of promotions and switched over to the counseling job. Now thanks to Jarvis Dupree, I'm fucked all over again."

"Not necessarily. You're clean, you have a solid education, and a good work history. Come on, let's see what kind of jobs are out there."

"I'm thinking I might go back to Boston," he said. "Florida's been nothing but trouble for me."

Yeah, great to spend time with you too. I opened a new browser window, and we started looking for jobs in Boston. "I'd like this one," he said, pointing to an agency that specialized in counseling teenagers grappling with issues like drug and alcohol dependency and sexual identity problems. A lot of the job involved administering tests to the kids, something Parker had enjoyed doing when he was in graduate school.

We went to their website, and he submitted an application. We found a couple of other jobs he could apply for, and by the time my stomach was grumbling for dinner he seemed to be a lot better.

He insisted that we could share his bed without problems, but I said I'd stay on the sofa, thank you very much. And when he finally went into his room to go to sleep, I felt like I'd passed a test of my own.

The next morning, I woke early and went for a long run around Parker's neighborhood, past Haitian kids in school uniforms walking to school, accompanied by mothers or older sisters, a pesticide company spraying the yard of an apartment complex, old men walking small dogs. I missed being by the beach, and wondered how long I would have to stay with Parker before I could go home.

Eddie was there, of course. Would he have moved out by the time I got back? There was no reason for us to live together anymore if we weren't a couple, and I couldn't face seeing him working everyday on the business I'd thought we were going to run together.

I would have to look for a real job, but now I'd sold my car, so I would have to be dependent on bus routes until I could get my finances together. Stupid, stupid. Why had I gone along with this crazy scheme? Was it Phil Sweet's fault for pushing us together? Eddie's for edging me out of the business?

Or my own for dreaming too big?

By the time I returned to Parker's apartment, I was tired and sweaty, but I was also energized. I couldn't depend on my father to push me the way he had directed me to Penn, for Eddie to love me when he didn't. It was up to me to make my life over.

Parker was in the kitchen in his underwear, snacking on potato chips and pomegranate juice. "I need to get back to my place," I said. "Can you drive me or should I call an Uber?"

"You can't leave me so fast," Parker whined. "I still need help applying for jobs."

He looked so pathetic I felt my resolve wobble. "Fine. But I need to apply too. We'll motivate each other."

He smiled. "Just like old times," he said. "You and me, together again."

"No, Parker. New times. Friendship, that's all."

"If you say so," he said, but I could tell he wasn't giving up.

I decided we'd search for jobs for each other for a while. Maybe he could come up with something I wouldn't think of. We spent the next two days, on and off, doing that. He convinced me to apply for a job at the FIU art museum even though I was sure I wasn't qualified, and I got him to consider applying for jobs in human resources at a couple of different corporations that were looking for people with his background.

I used Parker's car to run a few business errands, training a few new servers at an Italian restaurant and picking up some ingredients I needed. But I couldn't spend too much more time away from my kitchen, from all my supplies and equipment.

Eddie Gonzalez stayed at the back of my mind. Not just because he was in my apartment, and I wanted to go back there, but because I was curious to know what was happening with the business, even if he and Phil Sweet had moved me out of it.

Every so often I'd look at my phone and think about calling him. But Parker would distract me, or a new e-mail would come in from a client or a job prospect, and I'd push the phone away.

Chapter 29

Stupid

Without Darren around to distract me, I worked my ass off for the rest of the week, until I got a text on Friday from Phil Sweet that he'd flown in for a couple of days and wanted to meet as soon as possible. I responded right away and made plans to sit down at his office that afternoon.

"Thanks for coming in on such short notice," he said, as he shook my hand. "I'm heading back to Treasure Cay on the last flight out today."

He looked over my shoulder. "Where's Darren?"

"You said that you couldn't support his business, so he's out," I said.

"I didn't expect him to drop out of the project completely. Aren't you guys still a couple?"

"Don't think so," I said. "He's had some stuff going on with an ex, and we haven't spoken in a few days."

"This is not good. Phil sat down at his desk. "I thought you guys were a team. How are you going to manage without him?"

"I brought the numbers to show you," I said. "The business is actually a lot stronger without having to pay him a salary."

"What are you going to do about product development? Darren's the guy with the palate, isn't he?"

"He is. But that's not a unique skill. I can contract it out as I need."

Phil didn't look happy, but he said, "Let's see your numbers." I handed him a jump drive with the latest spreadsheets, and he opened it up. Neither of us said anything for the next couple of minutes as he flipped through the sheets.

"I don't know, Eddie," he said finally. "The numbers add up, but I don't get the same sense of passion that you guys showed when you first walked in my door. Where's the guy who buttonholed me at that venture capital event in New York last year? The one who was so enthusiastic about the possibilities of his business that he wouldn't let me walk away without tasting a cocktail?"

"I'm right here, Phil. And I'm still passionate about the business, but I've been through a lot of ups and downs lately."

"When you guys finally got together and pitched me your combined business, you were so eager you were finishing each other's sentences. Margarita's a great judge of character, and when she met you both on the boat, she was impressed. She said you guys are going to go far."

I felt the opportunity I needed slipping away. "And I can still go the distance on my own."

He shook his head. "I don't think so. I'm sorry, Eddie, but my initial instinct was right. You can't run this operation on your own. You need a partner like Darren, even if your company is focused on the cocktail business."

"I can't pay you back your investment right away," I said. "Because of the ginger recall I'm running my operation on fumes and the last of my savings. And we spent most of what you gave us on our trip to Ohio and the prototype development."

"I'm not a charity." Phil closed the spreadsheets and removed the jump drive. "I'll have my accountant put together a repayment plan."

He handed the drive to me. "If things change, get back to me.

Otherwise, I wish you luck, and I'll look forward to getting my investment capital back."

I took the drive from him, managed to spit out a thank-you, and walked out. I couldn't believe everything had fallen apart so quickly.

Fucking Darren Carter. Why had I ever trusted him? I was running on empty by that point, so I ducked into a Starbucks, ordered a venti helping of caffeine, and sat in the corner to wallow in my misery.

I had no place to live—I couldn't squat at Darren's apartment forever. Because I had to replace all the possibly tainted product for free, I had no revenue to speak of and I'd have to pay the production facility out of the last of my savings. I would have to move back in with my parents, my tail between my legs, and look for a job as a number-cruncher while I tried to salvage what I could of Cockteals.

It was a stupid name. Darren was right about that. And it was even stupider that I could imagine a future for myself as an entrepreneur. I was destined to be a regular wage slave, but I'd been out of the job market for a year, and all my contacts were in New York. And I didn't have an MBA, which seemed to be the entry level credential these days for jobs in corporate finance.

It was a long, sad drive from South Beach up to Darren's apartment, even more so because I knew he wasn't going to be there. Everywhere I looked I saw signs of failure—storefronts for rent, homeless people on the street.

My first memories of South Beach were of run-down Art Deco hotels along the beach, with old Jews in lawn chairs sunning themselves and waiting to die. Even then, the revival was happening, and those old hotels were being remodeled into hipster havens. The old Jews, the artists, and the Mariel refugees south of Fifth Street were already being pushed out, and by the time I was a teenager, fancy new hotels had opened, funky restaurants and shops lined Lincoln Road, and I walked past gay nightclubs, longing to be old enough to stay out late and hang out there.

By the time I returned home after four years at Penn and five in

New York, things had picked up. Investors renovated the hotels. Artists moved in, followed by restaurants and retailers, and after a long struggle the streets teemed with tourists and the smell of money mingled with the salt air once again. How did that happen? Was there anything I could do to mimic that revival?

I parked in Darren's space behind the apartment building and trudged upstairs. I dropped my messenger bag on a kitchen chair and slumped down. One of Darren's Penn T-shirts was draped over the chair opposite me, a visual reminder of his absence.

Things had been so much easier when we were in college together. All we had to worry about was studying and having fun. Sure, we were both thinking about the future, and keeping secrets from each other, but my path was clear—graduate, get a job, move into adulthood. Now I didn't know where I was going.

I picked up the shirt and sniffed it, catching a whiff of Darren's scent. I remembered coming back to his dorm room after a class one day where we'd been talking about the concept of grit, something one of the professors in the sociology department was writing a book about.

She said that the two key elements of grit were passion—being interested in what you were doing, feeling you had a purpose in doing it—and perseverance, which was all about repeated practice and a hope that you would succeed someday.

At the time, it seemed very simple. We were all high-achieving college students, at one of the nation's most prestigious universities. Of course we knew what it took to be successful, or else we wouldn't have made it to Penn.

I sat down at the table and thought about where my passion and perseverance came from. I was Latin, so passion was in my blood—I loved to drink cocktails, to dance, to have mind-blowing sex. I felt the rhythms of Cuban music in every fiber of my being.

Phil said he'd seen passion in my speeches about the cocktail business. It was true. I had a mission to bring my love of tea-based cocktails to the world. And I'd been persevering, fighting against lack of interest from bar owners, skepticism from venture capitalists, disdain from my own family.

Was I going to stop now? Where else would I find passion? What else would I care about enough to push like Sisyphus against a rock that kept falling back on me?

The only person I knew who had the same passion for tea was Darren Carter. But did he have the perseverance that was the other part of the grit equation? Sure, he'd struggled against the odds to start his business, and he'd been daring enough to move to Miami in order to work more closely with Sweet. Could we push each other to succeed, even if we weren't a couple?

I went back to the numbers I'd crunched, and began to work out where I could put Darren back into the business. I'd already recognized that I didn't have his palate, and that I'd have to contract out product development and testing, so it was easy to knock out the expense for a consultant and slot a salary for Darren back in.

I didn't know if he'd be willing to work with me again. I didn't know if we could be business partners without being lovers too. But if I wanted to persevere with my entrepreneurial dream, I had to have his help.

I thought about calling him a dozen times. But it was time to put a stop to our pattern of impulsive actions, to think everything through clearly before making a decision. So I didn't call him, and he didn't call me, and I wondered if he ever would again, if what I was doing was useless.

Persevere, I told myself. Keep going even if the odds were stacked against me. By the time I left for dinner at my parents' house on Sunday, I had put everything together in what I thought was a very persuasive package, to convince first Darren, and then Phil Sweet, that our business was a winner. But there was something missing, and I didn't know what it was.

It was a windy day, the palm trees along the causeway swaying restlessly. All the way out to Westchester, I went over my plans again and again. Fortunately, I was able to get home without consciously thinking about the directions.

"Where's Darren?" my mother asked when she opened the front door.

"Not here," I said. I leaned in and kissed her cheek. "Food smells delicious."

She frowned but didn't say anything more. Connie had brought Kyle back again, and everyone appeared to have assumed I'd have brought Darren again too. We danced around the issue, nobody coming out and saying anything.

"So how is your business?" my mother finally asked. "I thought you would bring Darren today, and we would hear more about what you are doing."

I looked down at my empty plate. "The guy we thought was going to fund us backed out, so I'm not sure Darren and I will be able to keep going."

"Maybe you will go back to school for your MBA," my father said. "You could come back here to live, save money while you study."

"You're always welcome here, mi amor," my mother said. "But what about Darren?"

"*Me gusta ese chico,*" Abuela said. "Even if he is un Americano."

"Yeah, lots of people like Darren," I said. "But without a business to run together..."

My father nodded. "*Claro que si,*" he said. "You will come back here, go back to school. Maybe you'll meet a nice Cuban girl. Connie, you have any friends for your brother?"

"Pa...pi," I said, drawing out the two syllables.

"What? I only want what's best for you."

My mother stood up. "Eduardito, you help me clear the table. Ramon, you wanted to ask Kyle about that bunion on your foot."

Connie groaned. "He's not a podiatrist, Mami."

"Whatever."

I helped her carry the dirty dishes into the kitchen. "You love him, don't you?" she asked, as she began rinsing the plates.

"I don't know, Mami. I thought maybe yes, but now with things falling apart..."

"Now is the time to show what you feel," she said. "Yes, love is easy when everything is *sol y rosas*. Do you know how many times I wanted to kill your father? Take a knife and cut out his heart? But I stayed."

"You and Papi love each other."

"Claro que si. But like I said, it is not always happiness. You work through the bad times, and you are both stronger."

Did that work for gay couples as well as straight? So many of my gay friends went through relationships like toilet paper—wiping their asses with one guy after another, breaking up at the first sign of trouble. The legalization of gay marriage had done as much damage as good, forcing gay men into heteronormative relationships like our straight role models. But what if that wasn't the way we were meant to be?

Sometimes there was too much testosterone between two gay men, without that female sensibility to calm things down. Was that what my problem with Darren was? Both of us wanting to be the alpha? Would that problem dog us forever? Did I want the settled domesticity my parents had, that Connie and Kyle were headed for?

I realized with a start that I did. And not only did I want that, I wanted it with Darren Carter.

I dried my hands on a dishtowel. "I've got to go, Mami. I'll talk to you this week."

"But we have flan for dessert!"

"Give my piece to Papi."

I said hurried good-byes to the rest of the family and strode out to my car, where I called Darren's number.

"What's Parker's address?" I asked, as soon as he picked up the phone. "I need to talk to you, and you need to come home."

Chapter 30

Champagne and Dreams

I was surprised to get the call from Eddie, but even more unexpected was how glad I was to hear from him. I gave him Parker's address and began to pack up my gear.

"You're going back to him?" Parker demanded.

"You knew that I would."

He sighed. "Yeah, but a boy can hope, can't he?"

"You're a good guy, Parker. You'll find a new job and a new guy, and you'll be great."

"From your mouth to God's ears," he said. "Though I think that HR gig with the cruise line might come through. That interview on Friday went well."

"You said." I nodded. "See, things are looking up."

It didn't take long to load my backpack and a couple of shopping bags. I kissed Parker on the cheek and said, "Don't take this the wrong way, but don't call me for a while, okay? I need to get my own life together."

"I understand."

I dragged my stuff downstairs and waited by the curb for Eddie to show up. Someone was grilling in the distance, the smell of barbecue floating on the air, and I heard kids squealing and laughing as they played. I couldn't wait to get back to my own place, to smell the salt water in the air. I even missed the salsa music my downstairs neighbor blasted.

But most of all I missed Eddie. My heart skipped a beat or two as I saw his car pull up. I threw my stuff in the back and hopped in beside him, and we both spoke at the same time.

"I'm sorry," I said.

"I'm sorry too," Eddie said. "But we need to talk. That's something we haven't done enough of." He put the car in gear and pulled out into traffic. "How's Parker doing?"

I took a deep breath. Yeah, we had to communicate, even if we both had to say things we didn't want to. "Better. We've been helping each other look for jobs."

"You need to work with me," Eddie said. "I can't do this without you, but our partnership is never going to work unless we communicate with each other. About business issues and personal ones too."

"Hold on," I said. "There's no part for me without the packaged tea component. So there are no business issues."

"There is. You have the tea knowledge, the palate, and the connections with tea connoisseurs."

We went back and forth on the drive over to the beach. What Phil Sweet thought, what Eddie had realized, what I'd figured out. We still weren't talking about the personal stuff, though. How could I work with Eddie, knowing that I loved him, if we weren't partners in life too?

Eddie parked in the alley behind the building, and he took the shopping bags from me to carry upstairs. "Let me show you the numbers I put together," he said, when we walked into the apartment.

We sat close to each other as we looked over the projections he'd made. I was occasionally distracted by the feel of his shoulder against mine as he pointed at something, the smell of his bay rum cologne.

"You put in a salary for me?"

"Of course. Like I said, I can't do this without you."

"But this is all your business, the cocktail side."

"And if we're going to expand, I need your help figuring out what to sell. You can handle the product development even if we're selling cocktail mixers."

"Do you think that Phil Sweet will fund us if we go back to him?"

"Even if he doesn't, there's nothing I want to do more than work with you. Live with you. Love you."

My mouth was dry. So Eddie wanted me too? This was all I'd ever wanted, wasn't it? To have a business I could care about, a man beside me who made me look forward to getting up every morning. And not just any man—Eddie Gonzalez.

I had to be sure, though. "The numbers look great," I said. "But we've been through a lot lately, Eddie. Do you think the mojo is still there between us?"

He took my hand and pressed it against his groin. His dick was as hard as mine. "That answer your question?"

"I don't know. I think I might need more evidence before I make a decision." I licked my lips and leaned in to kiss Eddie. It felt so good, so right, that I kept on kissing him as we fumbled with our shirts, knocking papers off the table in our eagerness to get together.

We stumbled out of our chairs and headed for the bedroom, shedding clothes as we went. By the time I flopped onto my bed I was naked, and so was Eddie. He jumped on top of me, and we were chest to chest, dick to dick, kissing as if we were both dying and the other was our only salvation.

He ground his dick against mine, and my pulse raced. "I want you inside me," I said, pushing him lightly away from me. When he backed off to get the condom and the lube, I scooted up against the pillows and raised my legs toward my shoulders.

"I'm never going to get tired of seeing you like that." Eddie moved in close to me, guiding his dick toward my hole with one hand, squirting lube in with the other. We were both too eager to do much preparation, and I leaned back and took a couple of deep breaths as he pushed against my hole.

And then he was inside me, and the endorphin rush through my body threatened to set me loose from this earthly plane. Eddie felt it too. I could tell from the glazed yet excited look in his eyes, the way he banged against my prostate, telling me how tight I was, how good I made him feel.

He wrapped his hand around my dick and began jerking me in the same rhythm he was plowing my ass, in and out, and I couldn't hold out for long. I was whimpering and moaning and crying out his name and shooting over my belly, the acrid scent of the cum filling our nostrils like poppers and setting him off so that he drove one last time into my ass and then spurted.

He was panting like a racehorse, sweat dripping from his shoulders, and I'd never seen a more beautiful sight.

He collapsed beside me. "We've still got it," he said. "And this is never going away, no matter what happens with the business."

I agreed with him.

Three days later we met with Phil Sweet once more. We were both nervous—he'd already said no to us a couple of times, and we both doubted there would be another chance back at the well if he said no once more.

His wife was with him in the office when we walked in, and she greeted us effusively, with kisses to both cheeks, as Phil watched from his desk. "I asked Margarita here today because I trust her judgment when it comes to people, and she's been a fan of both of you since you met on the boat."

That sounded promising. Eddie and I sat across from him.

"Are you both committed to working hard?"

I looked at Eddie, and he looked at me; then we looked back at Phil. "We are." I reached out for Eddie's hand. "Together, we can achieve anything."

"That's the enthusiasm I want to hear." Phil stood up and stretched his hand out toward us. "Gentlemen, we have a deal."

We both shook hands with him, and Margarita kissed us both again, and Phil brought a bottle of champagne out of a small refrigerator behind his desk. That celebration, though, was an extra bonus—I'd found my future with Eddie, and we'd spur each other on to everything we dreamed of.

Thanks for reading!

I'd love to stay in touch with you. Subscribe to one or more of my newsletters: Gay Mystery and Romance (http://eepurl.com/7UwFf) or Golden Retriever Mysteries (http://eepurl.com/7UwNv) and I promise I won't spam you!

Follow me at Goodreads to see what I'm reading, and my author page at Facebook where I post news and giveaways.

If you liked this book, please consider posting a brief review at your vendor, at Goodreads and in reader groups. Even a short review help other readers discover books they might like. Thanks!

I have some other ideas about books for this series, but right now this is the last one published. Here are all the books in the series:

Love on Site
http://amzn.to/1M1lUw5

Love on Stage
http://amzn.to/2qZmOkO

Love on the Boil

Thanks for reading!

https://amzn.to/2yepHaj

Love on the Map
https://amzn.to/2lcbOAc

Love on the Web
http://amzn.to/2sxfC1C

Love on the Pitch
http://amzn.to/2rMBkRo

If you liked these guys, you may also enjoy my collection of erotic short stories, which feature several of these guys. It's called *Three Lambs, Erotic Tales of a Gay Frat* (https://amzn.to/3brhiyJ).

Lambda Lambda Lambda, the all-gay fraternity at Florida University (FU) in Miami, is the setting for eleven hot new stories by master of gay erotica Neil Plakcy. Sexy college guys get it on with each other, with models and construction workers and security guards.

Meet the guys:

• Fitz, the preppy blond house manager, and his Chinese-American boyfriend Chuck, have an open relationship that often extends to other guys in the house.

• Larry, the skinny beanpole who's nervous about joining the frat —until he joins Fitz and Chuck in their bed.

• Wally, the swim team jock who runs afoul of campus security when he's caught pissing outside the physics building

• Nelson, the Jamaican engineering major with braids who has a crush on another Caribbean student, Aruba-born Willem

• Aspiring model Gavin, whose all-American good looks get him hired for a most interesting job involving fellow model Tate

• Joey, who discovers what Gavin can give him that his girlfriend can't – or won't

• Beautiful Manny, with coffee-colored skin and eyelashes to die for, who spends a little too much time eyeing the handsome, shirtless workmen on a new campus building site

• Football player Ryan, who disdains soccer and its players until he meets up with Orlando, who's more than his match in athletics

• Thom, who's unhappy about tutoring an angry football jock—until their sessions take an interesting turn

• Returning GI Eric who discovers he's got more than he expected in common with hippie roommate Barry

Join them all for some very hot times in colorful, multi-ethnic Miami.

To Marc. You are my honeybush tea, and I don't need sugar as long as you're by my side.

Acknowledgments

A big thanks to my tea tasters—Brittany and Kyle Roberts and Peter D'Ettore. And thanks to the *Pennsylvania Gazette,* Penn's alumni magazine, for the article on Owl's Brew, manufacturers of artisanal tea cocktail mixers, which triggered my imagination. This is the last of the books in the series originally published by Loose Id, and I appreciate all the help I received from my editor, Maryam Salim, and all the staff there who proofread, copy edited, designed great covers and helped get the word out about the books.

Of course, the biggest thanks go to the fans who have enjoyed taking this journey with me.

Contents

Ingram Content Group UK Ltd.
Milton Keynes UK
UKHW020633120623
423291UK00014B/656

9 798215 319543